MotoMy

Ghost Lights of Dry Brook

BOOK 2

SHERRI KUKLA

Join the Reader List!

Get an email whenever we release a new book and be one of the first to read the latest MotoMysteries stories! Send your name and email address to sherrikukla@gmail.com

www.sherrikukla.com
Facebook.com/motomysteries

GHOST LIGHTS OF DRY BROOK

Published by S&S Publishing, Inc.
www.sherrikukla.com
www.ssorm.com

ISBN: 978-1-7349484-2-4

You will seek Me and find Me
When you search for Me
With all your heart.
Jeremiah 29:13

In loving honor of my greatest
prayer warrior and champion
My Mother
Juanita Noah, Servant of God
12/17/34 - 7/12/19

In Memory of Emilie Elizabeth Puricelli
Her story inspired me

MotoMysteries

Book 1 - The Skeleton and the Lantern

Book 2 - Ghost Lights of Dry Brook

Book 3 - Phantom Ship in the Desert (Fall 2020)

The Christmas Miracle

A Christmas Mini-Mystery

Follow MotoMysteries on

www.sherrikukla.com

www.facebook.com/motomysteries

Chapter 1

Millie

"Mo-o-o-o-o-m-m-m-i-e-e-e-e-e-e-e!" Caleb's scream for his mother pierced the darkness causing Paisley's little brother Donovan to join in. Millie dropped the spotlight she held and rushed to clamp her hand over Caleb's mouth.

Her brother Jeremiah ran out of the bushes where he had been hiding and making animal noises.

"It's a joke, Caleb." Jeremiah whispered. But the tears streaming down his cheeks didn't stop.

"I feel like crying, too." Millie looked at her brother. "We're dead meat if Mom and Dad come out."

Paisley got Donovan to calm down, but they couldn't get Caleb to stop crying.

"I want my mommy!" His voice rose.

In the three months since Caleb moved in with the Andersons, Jeremiah and Millie had never seen him like this. Millie wrapped her arms around him.

Caleb clung to her, resting his head on her shoulder. Millie kept one eye on the house hoping her parents or Paisley's hadn't heard the commotion. They'd be in so much trouble for playing a trick on the little kids by pretending wild animals were close by.

"I want my mommy." Caleb kept crying. "I want my sissy."

Sissy? Millie looked at Jeremiah and then over at Paisley who knelt down, with her arm around her brother. None of them knew anything about Caleb having a sister.

He moved in with the Andersons when his mother went to jail. The Deputy Sheriff they'd become friends with introduced her parents to Caleb and told them about his need for a home. They had moved to this big property in the desert where their parents planned to give a home to kids who needed help. Caleb moved in a week after they arrived in the desert.

"Where is your sissy?" Millie rubbed his back, hoping to stop his tears. She glanced at the door again to make sure they were safe. So far it seemed their parents hadn't heard the commotion.

Paisley knelt on the ground close to her. Her little brother, now calm, leaned against her, ready to fall asleep.

Caleb grew quiet, but whispered again, "I want my sissy."

"Do you mean your mommy?" Jeremiah said, then leaned over to Millie. "Does he have a sister?"

"Not that I know of."

"Not my mommy!" His voice raised. He pointed across the desert. "My sissy, she's where the lights are."

Millie and the others looked where he pointed. Bright lights shone in their direction from off in the distance.

Chapter 2

Jeremiah

"Why do you think Caleb would suddenly start talking about a sister?" Millie and I sat at the kitchen table eating brownies after Paisley and her family left. Mom and Dad were putting Caleb to bed. What a relief we made it this long without them finding out about the problem outside.

"Beats me. But that is weird." Millie talked with her mouth full. Good thing Mom didn't see her. She could never get that girl to quit talking with food in her mouth.

"You know that's gross, don't you?"

She shoved another brownie in her mouth. "What's gross?" Her words were garbled and when she burst into laughter, she almost lost the mouthful of brownies.

"That's just wrong!" I looked away, but couldn't stop laughing.

Millie wiped her mouth. "I know, I know. I need to work on my manners."

"So back to this mysterious sister." I poured milk in both our glasses, waiting for her take on this. But instead of answers she fired another question at me.

"And why would he say she's by the lights?"

"Right." I took a big swig of milk, but rather than wiping the milk mustache off with my sleeve, I used a napkin to set a good example. "That was just some truck driving off Sunset Hill. What made him think it had to do with his sister?"

"Yeah, a sister we don't even know is real. And why did you call it Sunset Hill?" Millie shocked me when she wiped her own milk mustache off with a napkin instead of using her shirt like she did when Mom couldn't see her. Maybe there was hope for that girl.

"Haven't you noticed all the off road vehicles parked up there on a busy weekend, right about sundown?"

"I guess I haven't."

"Must be a good view of the sunset."

"Yeah," Millie nodded her head. "Let's ask Dad to drive us up there one of these days."

"Uh-huh, after he gets something to drive us in."

"Well," Millie said, "he promised we'd get a dune buggy after we moved in. It's time now."

"Time for what?" The deep voice startled us and we both jumped.

"Did I interrupt top secret conversation?" Dad smiled and reached for the last brownie.

"Time to get a dune buggy, Dad." Millie looked right at him. I was glad she answered his question. If there was something to talk about or ask for, it was easier to let her. She had a habit of just speaking up without thinking. All the time. And I was happy to let her do it. I'd get the answers, and she'd get the consequences if she was being too pushy or greedy or nosy or just about too much of anything. Which she often was.

"Well, before we talk about that dune buggy," Dad pulled out a chair and sat near us. "Let's talk about what happened outside tonight."

I wanted to glance at my sister but resisted the urge. And wouldn't you know it? This was one of those times the mouthy one stayed quiet. Dad looked from Millie to me. Waiting for an answer.

I was trying to decide if I should try the play-dumb-scenario like I don't know what he's talking about or just admit we made a bad choice in scaring the little boys and get the consequences over with. Before I made my decision, Millie opted for the play dumb routine.

"What do you mean, Dad?"

I knew by my dad's face that was the wrong thing to say. He didn't look happy with her less than honest answer. Man, was I glad I hadn't given that answer.

"Millie, you of all people should know what I'm talking about."

Chapter 3

Millie

"Why would I know more than Jeremiah would know?" Millie was ready to throw her brother under the bus. She wasn't going to take all the punishment when it was Jeremiah's idea to hide in the bushes and pretend to be a wild animal.

Dad sighed. "Why do I feel like there is more going on than I know about?"

Millie looked at her brother. "You tell," she said. Luckily she wasn't close enough to him so that he could kick her under the table.

"Do you two know something about Caleb having a sister that you're hiding from us?" Dad sounded stern. He was definitely tired of their vague answers. Millie wanted to laugh out loud with relief. This wasn't about them scaring the boys at all.

"No, Dad." Millie jumped at the chance to carry the conversation in another direction far removed from them playing a mean trick.

"That's what we were just talking about," Jeremiah said. "We've never heard anything about Caleb having a sister."

"Did Deputy Black say anything about other kids in the family when he helped Caleb move in?" Millie asked.

"No, nothing." Dad looked puzzled.

"So what did he say to you and Mom tonight?"

"We were getting ready to pray with him and Mom asked, like she always does, if he wanted to pray about anything." Dad took a glass out of the cabinet and poured some milk.

"And?"

"Ever the impatient one." Jeremiah looked over at Millie. "Let Dad get a drink."

She gave her brother a dirty look.

"And he usually says no," Dad continued. "But tonight he asked Mom to pray for his sissy. He said he saw her over by the lights tonight and he wants her to come live here."

"What did Mom say to him?" Millie asked.

"She said she'd pray about that and he was satisfied." Dad took another drink of his milk. "He drifted right off to sleep."

"Dad," Millie said. "Why did you say that I should have known what you were talking about?"

"Caleb said you were helping him to feel better," Dad looked over at her. "I guess he was sad because he was thinking about his sister."

Millie glanced at her brother with a quick eye movement, rather than turning her head, then looked back at her dad. But she didn't say a thing.

"Hey Dad," Jeremiah spoke up. "Can we have a campfire?"

She was glad for the change in topic. Even though she hadn't actually lied about what happened outside, she felt guilty.

Dad glanced at the clock on the wall. "I'll give you two about 30 minutes outside. Your mom and I have some things to discuss, so that will work out fine."

Millie looked over at Jeremiah. She was torn between being more interested in what her parents were going to discuss than going outside to have a campfire. But she knew it would look suspicious to stay inside now. She reluctantly followed her brother.

As they gathered kindling and firewood, the bright lights they saw earlier were back again. This time it seemed like they were coming right for them.

Chapter 4

Jeremiah

I dropped the wood and motioned for my sister. "Let's get closer to the fence line and see if that truck really is heading this way."

Millie set her wood down more quietly than I did and glanced behind her. I looked too, relieved to see that our parents were nowhere near the window looking out over the firepit.

We half ran, half walked through the brush and rocks, as we headed to the fence, but the truck that appeared to be coming our way, turned, heading a different direction.

"I think we're just spooked because of the weird way Caleb acted tonight," Millie whispered as we stopped to catch our breath.

"I think you're right." I pointed to the house. "Let's get back before they find out we're not building a fire."

"I'm sure Deputy Black would have told Mom and Dad if there were other kids," Millie said.

"Right, and even Dad said he didn't know about any."

"That kid hardly ever talks," Millie said, "and now to be so bold with all of us, insisting he has a sister, it's just weird."

"We need to talk with Deputy Black." I dropped the wood into the fire ring and lit the kindling.

"Maybe Paisley's family knows something about Caleb's mom." Millie poked the fire with a long stick she kept hidden from me. Someday I'd pay attention to where she puts it when she's not poking the fire. The fact she kept it hidden made me want to find it and poke the fire myself. With her watching.

"Why are you laughing?" She looked over at me.

"Because you're so protective about that stupid stick." I couldn't stop the laughter.

She poked the fire even more. "I love living out here." She settled back in one of the chairs and looked into the sky. "I love the stars, and the dirt and the trees . . . "

"I love riding my motorcycle every day before school," I interrupted.

". . . I love the moon and the sunrise and the hills . . ." she continued as if I hadn't even said anything.

"Millie, for Pete's sake! I get the point, you love the desert."

"Don't you?"

"I love riding my motorcycle every day, did you know that?"

We both burst out laughing. It felt so good to be done with all the troubles of trying to get this house and property and being chased by the bad guys, of worrying about Millie's adoption. It was a good feeling to just have all that over with and everything going good.

"Did you hear that?" Millie said.

"Hear what?"

Millie stood and was looking toward the edge of the property. "I can hear something, like a rumble." She stopped talking and stared intently.

I stood next to her but didn't see or hear anything.

"It sounds like a truck. A big truck. It's getting louder."

She was right. "Come on," I motioned and I started down the path toward our gate. "Let's go look."

She followed behind me a little ways until we saw the silhouette of one of the big gypsum mine trucks creeping along slowly in the moonlight, way out on the dirt road. I stopped walking and Millie bumped up against my side. She seemed scared.

"Why aren't his lights on?" she whispered.

"I don't know, and look how slow he's going."

"He shouldn't even be on that dirt road," Millie said. "They're usually on the highway."

We both watched as the truck rolled to a stop.

"He probably broke down." I turned and motioned for Millie to follow. "We better get back up to the firepit before our time is up."

"What do you think Mom and Dad wanted to talk about?" Millie asked as we walked back to the house.

Before I could answer, we heard Dad's voice.

"Millie? Jeremiah? Where are you two?"

We jogged the last little bit until we were in sight of the house. "Right here, Dad," I called out.

"It's time to come in. We need to talk to both of you."

Chapter 5

Millie

"Best part of homeschooling." Millie leaned back against the rough wood of the abandoned store and watched the sun come up.

Jeremiah took a drink of his orange juice before agreeing. "Yeah, setting our own schedule, and going riding every morning before schoolwork starts."

"You know, when I was in school," Millie looked at the brother she had come to love so deeply. "You know, before . . ." she choked up a little.

Jeremiah turned his head in her direction. "Before?"

"Yeah, you know, before this family."

That was one thing he never teased her about. He understood the challenges they'd each been through in foster care, hoping, praying for a family. It was something they probably would never joke about.

"I would hear kids talk about things they were doing with their families, and it was so hard not to be jealous." She scoffed. "Well, who am I kidding? I didn't even try not to be jealous. I didn't know then what the Bible says about it. I just flat out was jealous." She crushed her orange juice container and wadded the trash from her breakfast burrito. "And I was angry that I didn't have my own family."

Jeremiah took her trash and stuffed it into his fanny pack, ready to ride some more. Millie could tell he was listening intently. "But you have a family now, Mil. No reason to be angry. Just grateful."

"Even though I dreamed and hoped that one day I would," she looked over at Jeremiah. "I don't think I ever really believed it would happen."

He waited for her to continue. As if he could tell there was more to this conversation than just reminiscing.

Millie picked up her own fanny pack, breathed deeply and stared at the motorcycle in front of her. She had more to say, but it was hard to get it out. But she felt she had to tell someone. And Jeremiah was the only one she could tell.

"What is it, Millie?"

She appreciated his gentle voice.

"Well." She looked over at him. "This is going to sound mean, especially since I know what it's like to need a family. But I really like being the only daughter. I feel special. So important to Mom and Dad."

"You are important to them."

"What I'm getting at is, what if Caleb really does have a sister out there somewhere?"

Jeremiah waited. She appreciated that about him. He didn't rush her when it was really serious, he seemed to know she needed time to get the words together.

"What I mean is, I know how Mom and Dad are. I know they're following Great Grandpa's dream to give a home to kids who need one. And what scares me is, I don't want them to find Caleb's sister and give her a home too. You heard what they said last night. I know that's what they're going to try to do." She barely got the words out before tears fell.

Jeremiah handed her some crumpled napkins he found in his fanny pack, but stayed quiet while she cried.

"I'm ashamed to say it, but I don't want to share Mom and Dad with another girl. I want to be the only daughter. The important one."

Jeremiah smiled. "Oh, so it's okay for me to share them with another boy in the house?" He nodded his head. "I see how it is."

Millie smiled through her tears. "Yeah, I guess I didn't think about it that way."

Jeremiah stood and cinched his fanny pack around his waist. "Here's the thing, Millie," he looked right at her as he grabbed his helmet from where it hung on the handlebars. "God understands. He'll help you through it if that time comes." He pulled the helmet down over his head. "But we don't even know if there is a sister out there."

Millie wiped the last of her tears and joined her brother by the motorcycles. "Thank you for listening." She looked into Jeremiah's eyes. "And for understanding."

As she pulled her helmet on, something caught her eye behind the dingy windows of the abandoned store. She gasped.

"Jeremiah! Look!"

Chapter 6

Jeremiah

Millie took off running in her clunky riding boots and helmet before I could even get turned around to see where she pointed.

I saw nothing out of the ordinary, anywhere, except my sister disappearing onto private property clearly marked with a "No Trespassing" sign. She rounded the back side of the abandoned store and vanished.

I looked over at our motorcycles, then back in her direction and sighed. Loudly. Sometimes it was all you could do with that crazy sister of mine. I'm afraid she's on her own for this one. I wasn't about to leave our bikes sitting here unguarded for all the world to see. Well, not that all the world was driving down this road the old store was on. But I did see one car earlier. Oh and a big gypsum mine truck lumbered by us while we were eating the breakfast we brought along.

I straddled my motorcycle which was pointing in the direction Millie went. This way at least I could see if she ever decided to come back.

The sun rose higher and I knew we'd need to get back soon. Mom said no more than two hours and we were at least halfway through that much of our riding time, if not a little more.

"Millie!" I hoped she could hear me yelling. She probably expected me to follow her. But no way was I leaving my bike here. Just as I was about to yell again, I saw movement through the dirty window of the old store. I took a second look, but there was nothing. That was strange. I kept my eyes glued on that window in case it happened again. Maybe that was what Millie saw. Knowing her, she went around back looking for a way into the store. I sure hope she didn't find one. That would be breaking and entering. At least that's what they called it on the cop shows.

Speaking of cops. Suddenly there was one standing by my side. I looked at the man in uniform, wondering where he came from. I sure didn't see a cop car.

"Can I help you?" His words seemed nice. But the way he spit them out sounded anything but nice.

I looked around for the car I didn't hear and realized why. There wasn't one.

"Uh." I had no clue what to say and really wondered who this guy was. He had a uniform and a gun, but he sure didn't look like a Sheriff's Deputy. "Do you work with Deputy Black?"

"I'm asking the questions around here, sonny boy!"

"Excuse me, what did you want to know?" Something didn't feel right, but I played it safe hoping we could get out of here without trouble. Out of the corner of my eye, I saw Millie heading our way.

Mr. Uniform Guy must have seen her too. "Well, well, what have we here?" He turned in her direction, hands on his hips. "A trespasser!" He spoke the words like Millie had committed a major crime.

"You know I could impound this motorcycle for trespassing on clearly marked private property!"

Millie looked at me and I knew she didn't understand. "He means he can take your bike." I whispered, hoping the guy didn't hear.

"Who are you?" Millie challenged. "You're not in charge of this town. Let me see your badge."

Whoa, sister. Wrong thing to say. Big time wrong thing.

"You wanna see a badge, do you, little lady?" The man leaned his face close to her helmet, yelling. "Well, how about I just show you something else instead?"

He pulled out a set of handcuffs.

"Turn around, hands behind your back!"

Millie stood frozen in place. I couldn't move either. Was this really happening?

"Now!"

Chapter 7

Millie

"Jeremiah!" Millie whispered. "Do something!" The look on his face reminded her that she got them into this mess. "Please!" she tacked on to her hasty demand.

Jeremiah looked in her direction, then turned to the uniformed man.

"Excuse me, sir, uh, Officer."

"Yeah, what is it?" The man looked away from Millie and straight at Jeremiah.

"Well, would you please reconsider? My sister didn't think. She rushed off when she thought she saw a critter."

The man looked over to Millie. When he turned his attention back to Jeremiah, Millie's hopes lifted.

"She's always on the lookout for stray dogs who need help. If you let her go, I'll see to it that she never goes on that property again." Jeremiah seemed to grow more confident as the man listened. Millie had her doubts she could keep the promise

Jeremiah just made without consulting with her first. She knew she saw something move behind that dusty window.

A few scary moments passed while the man, who Millie really doubted was a cop, seemed to be deciding what to do, still dangling the handcuffs. "All right," he finally said. "You kids get on outta here. But don't let me catch you on that property again."

"Thank you, God," Millie whispered when her bike started on the first kick. She took off after Jeremiah so fast she nearly ran into his rear tire. She wanted to get away from this place. At least for now anyway. There definitely seemed to be something going on there worth exploring.

Jeremiah pulled over a few miles from the old store.

"Well, you just about got us in a world of trouble back there," he said as he pulled his helmet off.

Millie pulled a water bottle out of her fanny pack and sucked half of it down on the first gulp. Her mouth had gone completely dry when she saw the guy in the uniform waiting near Jeremiah.

"Who was that guy anyway? He sure didn't look like any cop we've ever seen around here."

"Oh, you mean in the three long months we've lived here?" Jeremiah grabbed her water bottle and finished it off. "It's not like we know every character in this town yet."

"Yeah, character, that sure describes him," Millie said. "I'm going to ask Deputy Black about him next time we see him."

"Oh no you don't!" Jeremiah stared at her.

"Why not?"

"What are you going to say? 'Who was that man who wanted to arrest me and impound my bike when I was trespassing?'"

"Oh, good point."

"Not to mention mouthing off to him." Jeremiah shook his head. "You need to learn to control that mouth of yours."

"I'll work on that."

"We better get back, our time must be about up." Jeremiah pulled his helmet on.

"Someone was inside that store." Millie said and then put her helmet on too.

"You heard what I told that officer." Jeremiah pointed his index finger at her.

"Yeah, yeah, I heard you," Millie said as she kicked her bike over.

"But that doesn't mean I'm going to do what you said," she whispered as she twisted the throttle and followed Jeremiah in the direction of home.

Chapter 8

Jeremiah

"Did you see something move through that window?" My sister whispered when we were sitting at the kitchen table doing schoolwork.

Mom and Caleb were in the living room working on his reading lesson. Even though he was seven years old he had never learned to read. We each took turns reading to him and encouraging him as he learned letters and sounds. He seemed excited about discovering he would be able to read books soon just like everyone else.

"Did you hear me?" My impatient sister poked my arm with the eraser on her pencil, bringing me back to the present, where instead of contemplating why a seven-year-old had never learned the alphabet, I had to put up with an impatient sister cooking up schemes that would get us in trouble. Like today, when she nearly got arrested. Which reminded me of something I wanted to talk to her about.

"I don't think that guy was really a cop." I looked over at her. "What do you think?"

"Well, you're most likely avoiding my question on purpose," she said, "but now that you mention it, there seemed to be something weird about him."

"Right." I tapped my pencil on the table as I thought back to what happened this morning. "Like he just suddenly showed up next to me and I never even saw a car. I don't even know where he came from."

"But he had that uniform on, and a badge and a gun," Millie said. "And for sure he had handcuffs." She grimaced, most likely at the thought of how close she came to feeling them clamp shut around her wrists.

"Can you imagine how much trouble we would have been in if he had impounded your bike?" I shuddered at the thought. "That would have been the end of our freedom for awhile."

"Why would he care if I was poking around that old ghost town of a store?" Millie squinted her eyes. She always did that when she was deep in thought, trying to unlock mysteries. I don't know how it helped her think. It was just plain funny looking if you asked me.

"I wonder how long that old store has been vacant," I said, not caring if I was interrupting her mental analysis of the facts. "Dad said he used to go there when he was a kid and get ice cream and candy when they were camping in the desert."

"Maybe he knows when it closed down, I'm going to ask him."

"Are you two deep in a discussion about social studies or science?" Mom opened the refrigerator and took out a pitcher of iced tea, then looked our way. We both gave her those deer-in-the-headlight looks wondering how much she heard.

"We were talking about our ride this morning." Millie recovered faster than I did. I was worried Mom heard us talking about the fake cop. "We ate our breakfast outside that old abandoned store. We just wondered how long it's been closed."

"As long as I've been coming to the desert with your dad," Mom said, pouring herself a glass of tea. She grabbed a cold water bottle out of the frig when she put the tea pitcher back. "Here you go, Caleb," she called out and then turned back to us. "I know your dad used to go there as a kid, but I don't ever remember it being open."

"Why does it just sit there empty?" I said. "Seems like someone would buy the place and open it again."

Caleb shuffled into the kitchen in his sock feet and took the water bottle. He was carrying a Dr. Seuss book under his arm and had a big smile on his face. "I'm going to learn to read this," he said softly, holding it up to show us. His voice was always so quiet you could hardly hear him. Except for last night, when he was so adamant about seeing his sissy. That was strange.

Mom patted Caleb on the head as he shuffled back out of the kitchen carrying his book and his water bottle. "I'll be right there, Caleb," she said.

"I heard once there was some strange goings-on where that store was concerned." Mom got back to my question.

Millie looked over at me. I could see her out of the corner of my eye, but I kept my eyes on my mom.

"You'd have to ask your dad more about it when he gets back from his trip." She picked up her tea glass and took a sip before she added, "But if I remember the story right, someone died there many years ago."

CHAPTER 9

Millie

"A murder?! There was a murder at that store?"

"Millie, shush," their mom said. "You'll frighten Caleb and I didn't say it was a murder."

"Well you said someone died there. What else could have happened?"

"How about they got sick and died?" Jeremiah said. "How about they were old? How about they had a heart attack?"

"Okay, okay," Millie said, "I get the point."

"You two get back on your schoolwork," Mom said as she left the room. "Your dad can answer questions for you when he gets home."

Millie waited until she was out of sight. "I'll bet it was a murder," she whispered.

Jeremiah was making notes in his science workbook. He looked up at her. "Millie, you heard Mom. She said it wasn't a murder."

"No, she did not say that."

"We both heard her," Jeremiah sighed. "You can be so exasperating."

"Well, that's a nice big word for today. Is that on your spelling test?" But before he could answer she continued. "She never actually said the words 'there was no murder.' She said 'I didn't say there was a murder.'"

Jeremiah looked at her and shook his head.

"Big difference," Millie insisted. "Big. And the fact that she didn't tell us any other way the person died, tells me it very likely was a murder and she didn't want to talk about it."

"Whatever." Jeremiah looked back down at his science workbook. He seemed to be done with the conversation.

Millie was far from finished with this topic.

She opened up her binder and began scribbling notes on a blank sheet of notebook paper.

Jeremiah glanced over at her. "Finally, you're doing what Mom told us."

"Uh-huh," she said without looking up.

She kept writing. Her list was growing.

Ask Dad when the store closed

Ask dad about the murder

Find out when the murder happened

Find out who the fake cop was

See if Paisley knows any of these answers

"What subject are you working on?"

Jeremiah's question interrupted her focus and she tried to ignore him as she continued writing.

Ride bicycle over to store and try to see inside (maybe Paisley will go)

"Millie!" Jeremiah whispered.

She looked up to see him staring at her. "What?"

"I asked you what subject you're working on."

"Why? What's it to you?"

"I've just never seen you so eager to make notes when you're studying."

"Oh," she chewed on the pencil's eraser as she studied the list. Then she noticed he was still staring at her. "English," she said.

“Oh, that’s interesting.” His monotone answer didn’t match his words.

“Why, what’s the big deal?” Millie said.

“Just that you have your Social Studies workbook open, but you say you’re working on English.”

Jeremiah reached toward her binder, but Millie shoved it farther away.

“I’m working on my spelling words,” she said.

“Uh-huh, sure.” He stared at her. “But remember, you just about got arrested today.”

“By a fake cop,” she said.

“Curiosity killed the cat you know,” Jeremiah whispered.

“I’m not a cat,” Millie said.

Chapter 10

Jeremiah

What a relief to stand outside and watch my mom drive off with my sister and Caleb in the car. I was ready for a break from her yakking about that old store.

Caleb waved from the back seat, a big smile on his face, as he headed off to play with Paisley's little brother, Donovan, his new best friend. It took about 15 minutes to get to the Ridge Riders Lodge from our place, where they lived. Paisley also homeschooled. Some days she worked in the store of her parents' lodge after school, but today they had invited both Millie and Caleb over to visit.

Well, they invited me, too. But spending the afternoon listening to two girls obsessed with conjuring up a new mystery was not my idea of fun. Not when I had a motorcycle I could work on. Unless they were going to take the family dune buggy out. I hadn't thought of that when I declined the offer.

"Too late now," I said as I headed toward Dad's shop. Thankfully, he left the keys for me when he took off for the city yesterday.

"Well, now, lookie here who I jist ran into!" The booming voice echoed through the shop just as I got all the lights on and opened my tool box.

"Minnesota Mike!"

"Who else did you expect to come sneakin' up on you like that?" The Santa Claus look alike came into the shop and gave me a bear hug.

"It's good to see you. Where have you been?" Even though we had only known him for a few months, it seemed like he'd been a family friend for years.

"Where else, but out looking for more adventure!" He reached in his pocket, bringing out a folded paper. "Lookie here at this beauty!" He shook the paper open.

I stepped toward him, looking at the tattered paper with pinholes in it. Must have been on a bulletin board somewhere. It was a handwritten ad with a photo of a red four-seater dune buggy.

"Hey, are you going to get that?" I took it out of his hand to get a better look. Minnesota's face reflected the excitement I felt. I knew he'd be taking us for rides if he got it. "Look at that light set-up," I said before he could answer.

"Boy, we could see halfway across the desert driving around at night in that beauty, couldn't we now?" Minnesota Mike agreed. "Where's your pops? I figgered on taking him with me to check this here thing out. Ya know, get his opinion. He's one right smart guy."

"Dad's not home, he went to the city to visit Mr. Smith."

"That the older feller that sold you the property?"

"Yes, but Dad and Mom say he gave us the property."

"Right generous thing to do," Minnesota Mike said. "I think he was eager to see yer folks use the land to help kids."

"Mom and Dad want him to come for a visit. They said he misses the desert."

"It'll do him a world of good to spend some time with you folks." Minnesota Mike folded the paper and slipped it back in his pocket.

"Well now, I guess I'll jist have to go look at this beauty by myself. It's only about a half hour drive from here." He turned to leave, then stopped and looked back at me.

"Unless you know anybody else what might want to tag along." He let out one of his belly laughs and turned back toward the door.

CHAPTER 11

Millie

"Did your parents find out about the wild animal trick we played on the boys?" Millie asked her new best friend as they headed up to her bedroom. She had become instant friends with Paisley several months ago when her family stayed at the lodge that Paisley's parents owned. Once they moved to the desert, the girls became inseparable.

Paisley breathed a sigh of relief. "Thankfully, no."

"I don't know why we did that. It was mean," Millie said. "Guess I'm not used to having a little brother. But that's no excuse."

"Caleb's a sweet kid."

"That reminds me, I wanted to ask if you know anything about his family. What do you think about him talking about a sister?"

"I asked my mom." Paisley shook her head. "She knows nothing about Caleb's family, but maybe you could talk to the deputy. I bet he would know."

Millie reached into her backpack and pulled out her list. "Yeah, that's what Jeremiah and I were talking about. But I have other questions for you, too." She looked up and smiled at her friend. "You're my information source, you know, since you've lived here your whole life."

"Okay, what's up?"

"First, what do you know about that abandoned store a little way off the highway? I can't remember the name of the road it's on."

"Oh, you must be talking about the old trading post. It's on Monument Road."

"Yeah, that's the one. How long has it been closed down?"

"Since before I was born."

"My mom said someone died there." It tempted Millie to say it was murder, but she wanted to get Paisley's take on it without influencing her. She didn't know why, but she hoped it was a murder. That seemed more mysterious and exciting.

"I never heard that." Paisley went to her bookcase. "But I never asked." She pulled out a book and returned to the bed where they both were sitting.

"What's that?" Millie asked.

"It's about southwest desert history." She shuffled through pages, then stopped on the table of contents. "Maybe something is in here about our town."

Millie scooted next to her so she could see the contents page. "Look right there," she pointed. "Is that it?"

"Ye Olde Dry Brook Trading Post," Paisley read out loud. "That's what they called it." She flipped to the page. She must have been reading faster than Millie or skipping parts of it because suddenly she looked up, her eyes big and mouth open.

"Wow, Millie, listen to this!"

Chapter 12

Jeremiah

"Woo-hoo are we going to have a blast in this thing!" Minnesota Mike bounced in his truck seat as we drove down the highway towing a trailer carrying a flashy looking red four-seater dune buggy. Room for me, Dad, Mike and Millie. I couldn't wait for Dad to get home from his trip to give us permission for a ride.

Our windows were down and Mike's beard and hair were blowing in the wind as he bounced around in his seat while he drove. This guy was more excited than me.

But then I thought of a problem.

"Hey, Mike." He glanced over at me, then back at the highway, still wearing the biggest smile I ever saw on this old guy. "Where will you keep the buggy? You don't even live around here."

"Well, sonny boy," he glanced over and smiled even bigger, if that's possible. "There's another thing I been meaning to tell you and your folks."

This sounded exciting.

"I bought me a right cozy trailer in that nice place over where your friend lives."

"At the Ridge Riders Lodge?" I asked.

"That be the place, sonny boy. I am now a permanent resident of this little town. And wouldn't you know it? There is room to park my truck and new buggy right next to my trailer."

"That's the best news ever!"

"I agree," Minnesota said. "I guess my traveling days are over. I'm having too much fun hanging out with you and your family. You kids seem to have a knack for finding adventure. So what's the point of me driving all over the country looking fer what I can find right here with the likes of you?"

I turned to stare at the trailer and buggy. "Yeah, and I see lots of future adventure following right behind us. I can't wait to go for a ride in that buggy."

"You and me both, sonny boy. We'll wait for yer pops to get home and we'll plan an outing real soon like."

The truck jerked hard to the right. I turned to see what happened, as a car almost sideswiped us. Minnesota Mike held on tight to the steering wheel as we hit rough dirt on the side of the road while avoiding the oncoming car.

"What's that guy thinking?" Minnesota's voice sounded strained.

"That scared me! I was looking at the trailer and didn't see it coming."

"You didn't get a look at the feller driving?" Minnesota glanced over at me, then back at the road. "Almost looked like he were a cop the way he dressed, but that shore weren't no cop car."

"I caught sight of a uniform," I said. "It almost reminded me of the guy who tried to handcuff . . ." I stopped before I gave away the trouble Millie got us into this morning.

I stared straight ahead, but out of the corner of my eye, I saw Minnesota Mike look over at me. No way was I going to make eye contact. First off, I was a bad liar, and second, this was Millie's secret too.

"What's that sonny boy? You stopped talking awful fast."

The car was quiet except for the sound of the wind whistling past us through our open windows as we sailed down the highway. I wasn't sure where to take the conversation next. I didn't want to lie to Mike, but I didn't want to tell him what happened either.

"Were ya gettin' ready to say it's the guy what was going to handcuff Millie?"

My head jerked in his direction, and I'm sure my eyes were bulging out. "How did you find out?"

Minnesota chuckled. "Well, I didn't know for sure."

He looked over at me and smiled. "But I sure know now."

CHAPTER 13

Millie

"The proprietor of Ye Olde Dry Brook Trading Post closed the business and left the area within days of his partner's untimely death. He was never known to return. As of the writing of this book, Ye Olde Dry Brook Trading Post stands deserted and abandoned. Who knows what secrets are hidden in the walls and halls of the beloved store that served travelers and locals for decades?" Paisley read the passage aloud and looked at her friend.

Millie stared, eyes and mouth wide open. "Wow!"

"You're not kidding, 'wow!'" Paisley said. "So your mom was right, someone died there."

"Untimely death, it said." Millie grabbed the book from Paisley and re-read that portion. "Untimely! That could mean murder!"

"Murder?" Paisley looked startled. "Why would you assume that?"

"Well, he couldn't have been sick. That wouldn't be unexpected."

"He could have had a sudden heart attack, or maybe a car accident," Paisley said.

"And it could also have been murder."

"Why are you so sure it's murder?"

Millie shrugged. "I don't know, I guess because it's more exciting." She looked over at her friend. "It's the stuff legends are made of."

"You're right about that," Paisley said. "So how do we find out?"

That's what Millie loved about Paisley. Instead of acting like her ideas were stupid or weird like other so-called friends from her past, she went along with Millie's adventures and even more important, Paisley was also excited about them. "It's not only the past we need to find out more about," Millie whispered.

"What do you mean and why are you whispering?" Paisley whispered.

Millie smiled. "Why are you whispering too?"

The girls were both laughing when Paisley whispered again. "I guess because you are."

"Well, I'm whispering because I don't want anyone but you to hear me." Millie stood and walked across the room to the closed bedroom door. She opened it and peered out to see if anyone was in the hallway. Satisfied they were alone she sat back down on the bed.

"Well?" Paisley said.

"Something is happening at the store right now."

"Why do we have to whisper about it?" Paisley said.

"Because," Millie leaned closer. "I almost got arrested today."

"You what?" Paisley blurted out.

Millie put her hand over her friend's mouth. "Shush, you'll get me in trouble. Big trouble. And the worst part would be I couldn't go back to investigate."

"You better start at the beginning."

After Millie filled her in on the happenings of the morning, she finished with a question. "Will you go with me to get a look in the windows, since I can't count on Jeremiah to help?"

"When and how are we going?"

"I've got it all figured out. Spend the night on Friday. Saturday morning we'll go for a bicycle ride. That will give us the perfect opportunity." Millie said.

"That's a great plan. Then we can also watch for the lights together on Friday night."

"What lights?" Millie asked.

Paisley looked surprised. "You mean you haven't heard about them?"

"No, what lights?"

Paisley looked at Millie for a minute before she spoke. "I'm not sure I should tell you what kind of lights."

Chapter 14

Jeremiah

I held my breath, waiting for Minnesota Mike to speak. Wondering how I would answer. How could he have known about Millie almost getting arrested?

The desert rushed by my open window. I stared straight ahead. The brisk wind blowing in the window helped cool my burning face. I kept waiting for him to say something else. My heart beat hard, wondering how much he knew.

"It shore got quiet in here, did you notice that, sonny boy?" Minnesota Mike chuckled.

Nothing seemed funny to me.

"Tell you what, sonny boy, I can take a hint. I know when someone doesn't want to talk about something. How's about we move on to another topic?"

My entire body relaxed. What a relief. For now, at least. I know how sly that old man could be. I knew he would catch me off guard and spring it on me. "Okay," I said after much thought. "I like that idea."

"You and that sister of yours been checking out the ghost lights?"

I turned to see if this was some kind of joke. He wasn't laughing. Just staring at the road as he drove.

"What are you talking about?"

"Well, they been around these parts for decades, I been told. I jist now heard about them the other night."

"Why did you call them ghost lights?"

"Don't rightly know why folks call them that, maybe cause they're spooky looking." Mike clicked his blinker on and slowed the truck.

I still wanted to talk about the so-called ghost lights, but now another question popped into my mind. Like, why did he turn here on Monument Road? This wasn't the way to our house.

"Where are we headed?"

He chuckled and looked over at me. "This road a little familiar to you?"

My body tensed. I thought at least he'd wait a couple days before he tried to get me to talk about Millie's near arrest again. Now we were heading right to the scene of the crime, as they say.

I tried to think of some nonchalant comeback, but I'm bad at lying and anyway, even if I had something to say, I couldn't have gotten the words out. I wasn't used to feeling awkward around Minnesota Mike. He was one of those guys that just puts you at ease. Except for now, while approaching the abandoned store.

I closed my eyes, waiting for the truck to come to a stop, so he could pry the truth out of me, right here where it all happened. Once Dad and Mom found out, we'd never get to ride off the property by ourselves again.

"Let's go check out where those spooky lights might be comin' from." Minnesota's words interrupted my fretting.

Relief flowed through me as the truck passed by the old store. I couldn't resist turning around to look.

What a mistake that was.

CHAPTER 15

Millie

"What do you mean you shouldn't tell me what kind of lights?" Millie's voice raised. "Why even bring it up then?" She stood to leave.

"Millie!" Her mother's muffled voice through the closed bedroom door provided an escape from Paisley.

"I gotta go." She hurried to open the door. "Be right down, Mom."

She no sooner got the words out than the door banged shut. Stunned at the force Paisley used to slam the door, Millie stared at her friend. "Why are you so upset with me?" Paisley said.

"Because you're reminding me of girls where I used to live. All the time keeping secrets. Like I'm not smart enough, or cool enough, to be told."

"It's not like that." Paisley held her palm against the door, keeping it closed. "I would never treat you like that, Millie."

Millie shoved her hand aside and tried to open the door. "Well, you sure coulda fooled me." The words shot out of her mouth as she squeezed through the barely open door and approached the stairwell.

She felt she stepped back in time. Back to where the kids were mean. Always mean. The girls in particular. Maybe it was all a glorious dream, that she'd discovered a genuine best friend. Unwanted tears formed. As she lowered her foot to the first step, Paisley's loud whisper caught her off guard and she almost lost her balance.

"Ghost lights!" The whispered words blasted out of her mouth like cannon fire.

Millie looked back at her. "Ghost lights?" she repeated. "What are you talking about?"

"That's what they call the lights." Paisley said.

Millie stepped back up onto the landing outside Paisley's bedroom. "Why couldn't you tell me before?"

"I wasn't sure how you'd feel about it."

"How could you not know?" Millie gave her friend thumbs up accompanied by an enormous smile. "I'm always up for adventure, especially a spooky one."

"They say the lights have been around a hundred years," Paisley said. "Come see." She went back into her room. "I'm sure it's in the book."

"Bring it when you come over. My mom's waiting for me," Millie said. "But why haven't we seen them before if they've been around that long?"

"I don't know. I've never seen them as long as we've lived here, which is practically my entire life. But now people are talking about them."

"What are they saying?"

"Millie, we're waiting!" Her mom's voice drifted up the stairwell.

"Come on, quick, tell me," Millie started down the stairs.

"Ghost lights," Paisley whispered as she followed her downstairs. "I don't know any more."

"Then how do you know how long people have been talking about them?"

"Oh," Paisley whispered when they saw the little boys and their moms waiting at the bottom of the stairs. "I guess I know a little more."

Chapter 16

Jeremiah

Millie would never forgive me for not telling her what I saw as we sailed by. But if I told her, she'd return to the store for sure. Why did we have to take this road?

"What are you so fidgety about, sonny boy?" Minnesota Mike reached out to the dash and turned the radio on.

The static gave me time to answer while he searched for a station. I hated feeling nervous and scared. This day should have ended on a high note going with Minnesota Mike to pick up the cool old dune buggy. But it sure didn't seem so fun right now. This was almost worse than seeing the guy threaten to handcuff Millie.

"See somethin' that shook you up back at the store, did you now?" Minnesota said.

"Why do you ask?" I tried to sound casual, but figured he heard the shake in my voice.

"Because I saw something too."

My head jerked in his direction without me meaning to. "You did?"

"Sure did, sonny boy, and I'll tell you, something ain't right."

I turned and look back over my shoulder, but we were too far past the store. "Who were those people?"

"Not sure, but I know one thing. They don't belong there."

"Maybe they're buying the place."

"Well they got a mighty suspicious way of acting if they're looking to buy the place." Mike continued trying to tune in a station as he drove.

"Were they yelling at those kids?" The scene etched itself in my mind. One man stared at the truck as we drove by. Another tried to herd children into the old store.

"I couldn't tell for shore," Mike said. "I just knowed they's ain't supposed to be anybody prowling around."

"How do you know?" I felt calmer discussing the strange happenings. The strange thing was, I hadn't seen anything definitely wrong going on. But something didn't seem right.

Mike got a radio station tuned in, sort of. We heard music now mixed in with the static. "There now, that's what I'm talking about!" He seemed pleased with his accomplishment. And he also used that minor accomplishment to ignore the question I asked.

"Mike," I said. "How do you know no one should be there?" He looked at me, then back at the road. "Well now, sonny boy, some things you just can't talk about."

Chapter 17

Millie

"I thought Friday would never get here," Millie said as the girls settled back in their sleeping bags.

"I can't believe your dad is letting us sleep out here by ourselves." Paisley fluffed her pillow then laid back, gazing at the stars.

"That's what he built this tower for. So we could have outdoor sleepovers and be safe from nocturnal desert critters roaming around."

Paisley tore open a bag of chips and offered some to Millie.

"Now tell me about these ghost lights." Millie's words were muffled with her mouthful of chips.

"Your brother is right. You have the worst manners!"

"Hey, you offered me the chips when you knew I had a million questions for you." Millie reached into the bag and stuffed her mouth again.

"Okay, I'll talk," Paisley said, laughing. "You just chew quietly and listen."

Little puffs of crunched up chips slipped out of Millie's mouth as she tried to chew while laughing.

"So the story goes back to the 1800s," Paisley said. "My dad and I looked it up on the office computer the other day after one of our guests mentioned something about seeing ghost lights."

"What do you mean, one of your guests? How many people were visiting you that day?" Millie interrupted.

"No, silly," Paisley hit her on the shoulder. "That's what we call the people who stay at the lodge."

"Why don't you just call them customers?" Millie asked.

"It's hotel etiquette, my dad says."

"Oh, okay, I guess that makes sense. So what did you and your dad discover?"

"A stagecoach driver first told the story of the ghost lights back in the 1800s. He called them 'fire balls.'"

"Sounds like fireworks," Millie said.

"Same thing I thought."

"I wonder if they had fireworks back then?"

"Yes." Now it was Paisley's turn to munch on chips while she talked. "Fireworks were first used by the Chinese back in the second century and the first we could find mention of their use in the United States was in the early 1600s."

"You sound like an encyclopedia."

"Well, it's just that my dad and I had the same question about the possibility of the ghost lights being fireworks, so we checked that out too."

"If that's all they were, that takes all the excitement away." Millie was ready to move on to another topic, like the history of the abandoned store. She was sure there was a murder mystery waiting to be solved.

Paisley continued. "It said the lights rose in an arch and then returned to the ground. That doesn't sound like fireworks."

"No, I guess it doesn't." Millie was growing weary of the lights story but she didn't want to be rude since Paisley seemed so interested in the lights. "Why do you think we're going to see these lights from a hundred years ago?"

"There have been some sightings lately and people are saying the ghost lights are back." Paisley shivered and burrowed down in her sleeping bag. "It's so cold. Do you think we'll last all night?"

Millie zipped her bag up the rest of the way. "We better if we want a chance to see the spooky lights."

The girls grew quiet as they laid back and studied the night sky. There wasn't a cloud to be seen and thousands of stars twinkled, but nothing that could be called ghost lights.

Millie felt herself nodding off when she heard a loud rumble in the distance. She kept her head down on her pillow but turned toward Paisley to see if she had fallen asleep. Her eyes were open wide.

"Did you hear that?" Paisley said.

Chapter 18

Jeremiah

Earlier it seemed tonight would be the perfect opportunity to be miserable. I still hadn't told Millie about the people at the abandoned store the other day. If I did, she would hound me endlessly, wanting to know every single detail, right down to what color shoes they wore. Not to mention the more serious problem it would create. She'd been itching to get back and explore. Knowing what I saw would have sent her running to investigate.

I hated keeping secrets. Especially because I'm so bad at it with my sister and I feel so guilty around my parents. My big plan for the evening, once I heard about the sleepover with Paisley, was to hide in my room with a good book. That way the girls wouldn't talk to me about abandoned stores or ghost lights. Whatever that silly wives' tale was, I didn't even know.

Honestly, I think Minnesota Mike was pulling my leg when he drove down Monument Road, supposedly to check out the lights. We got nowhere with that escapade. More likely he wanted to get a reaction out of me when we drove past the store.

And boy, did he get a reaction. But I don't think it was what he was expecting. Even he seemed surprised seeing people there.

Even if he did try to trick me, I didn't care anymore. He was about to rescue me before Paisley arrived. And since Millie would have a friend here, I got the privilege of being the only one to go out on a night ride in Mike's new red dune buggy.

Now we sat atop one of our favorite desert hills and surveyed all of our property and the surrounding desert. We could see campfires across the highway. Off road vehicles drove all around, lights bouncing up and down as they hit the whoops. Some folks sailed up the big sand hill, challenging each other to get to the top the fastest.

"You know, Mike," I pulled off my helmet and looked over at him. He did the same. "I never imagined we'd really live out here in this off road paradise."

"Well, now, doncha know," he smiled over at me and then took a long swig out of his water bottle. "This is the living, that's fer sure." He patted the aluminum dash panel of his buggy as he switched the engine off, then let out one of his trademark belly laughs. "And this little darlin' makes the off road living even better."

"It sure does. Hey, when are you going to let me have a try at driving?"

"Well now, sonny boy, you'll have to take that up with yer dad, doncha know."

Minnesota Mike was one fun guy, but sometimes not fun enough. I thought I could get him to let me try driving without getting permission. But then again, if he was the type to let me do stuff without my parents knowing, they wouldn't trust him. I guess it's all for the best.

"Hey," he whispered and pointed to some movement off in the distance.

"What do you see?" I whispered back. I didn't know why we were whispering.

"That big mine truck, jist sittin' on the dirt road."

I almost didn't notice the truck in the darkness. All the lights were off. Usually lights glowed all around those trucks.

"That ain't right." Minnesota pulled his helmet back on. "No." He shook his head as he fired up the engine. "Jist ain't right."

CHAPTER 19

Millie

"It sounds like a big truck," Millie whispered.

Paisley laughed. "Why are you whispering?"

Millie sat up and shrugged. "I don't know." She joined in the laughter. "I guess I always whisper when I think there's something mysterious going on."

"Shh," Paisley said as the rumbling grew louder.

"Yeah, I think it's a big truck out on the road. It must have shut the engine off and now started it up again."

"It sounds like a gypsum mine truck." She looked at Millie. "Why would it be around here?"

Millie rummaged in her backpack. "I don't know, but this isn't the first time. Aha!" She pulled out a pair of binoculars, then stood and peered intently through the lens.

"What do you see?" Paisley whispered. "Let me look."

"Hold on! I haven't even found it yet."

"Maybe you're not looking in the right direction."

“I’m looking in the direction Jeremiah and I saw the truck.”

“You’ve seen one out here before and didn’t tell me?” Paisley said.

“Well, it didn’t seem that important.” Millie swept the area with the binoculars. All the while, the rumbling continued.

“When was it?”

“That night we scared the boys. Ah! I found it!” She pulled the binoculars from around her neck and handed them to Paisley. “Look in that direction.” She pointed. “You can barely see it because of the trees along the road.”

“Maybe God was trying to scare you guys that night.” Paisley laughed as she pulled the binocular strap over her head. “You know, payback for scaring the boys.”

“Yeah, never thought about that,” Millie said. “The Bible says you reap what you sow.”

“Oh, yeah!” Paisley said. “I see it. He’s just sitting there with no lights on.”

“Jeremiah and I thought maybe he was broke down when we saw him the other night.”

“If he was broke down, why would his engine still be running?”

“I don’t know, we didn’t think that far, because our dad called us. We had to hurry back to the house.”

As the girls talked, the truck slowly started rolling. “Look.” Paisley handed the binoculars back to Millie. “He’s starting to move, but still no lights on.”

The engine rumbling grew faint.

“Does your dad know anyone who works at the gypsum mine?” Millie asked as the girls settled back into their sleeping bags.

“Yeah, Hank does. He comes in the store a couple times a month.”

Millie rustled around in her backpack again, pulling out her notebook and pen.

“You carry everything in there!” Paisley said.

“Don’t have the kitchen sink.” The girls laughed as Millie jotted down: Ask Hank about truck on her list of things to do.

"Well, this sure was a big disappointment for seeing the ghost lights tonight." Paisley snuggled into her sleeping bag, eyes closed.

Millie couldn't respond right away, stunned at what she saw heading their way.

"Uh, maybe not. Paisley, look over there!"

CHAPTER 20

Jeremiah

My teeth chattered as Mike floored the gas pedal and we flew down the hillside toward the big truck. Whether from cold, excitement or fear, I didn't know. I wanted to ask what he had in mind, but knew he wouldn't hear. And even if he could, he probably wouldn't answer. Fully focused, he drove the bouncing car over rocks and through ruts, heading in the truck's direction.

Once down on flat ground we didn't have the bird's-eye view the hilltop gave us, so it was hard to pinpoint where to go. But the bigger problem, at least in my mind, was what if we caught the truck? It could be dangerous.

I hung on as Mike kept the pedal floored. We slid around corners as he maneuvered through bushes and along trails that he must have hoped would lead us to the mysterious truck.

Finally, with no luck, he slowed and headed to Sunset Hill. It was long past sunset, so we were the only ones there. This hill wasn't as tall as the other one, but since it was closer to the highway, we could still see across the road where off road vehicles were cruising around in the desert. On busy weekends, adventurous ones were out all night long. It was fun lying in bed at night listening to the roar of the vehicles exploring the desert.

"Lookie there," Mike shouted over the sound of the buggy engine.

I turned my head in time to see a big mine truck rolling down the highway. "Is it the same one?" I shouted back.

"Don't rightly know fer sure." He rubbed his chin under his helmet. I noticed he did that when he was thinking hard about something.

"The lights on that truck look different from the mine trucks I've seen."

He nodded his head. "You're right about that, sonny boy. Unfamiliar pattern. Some of the lights on top are different colors, too."

"The rest of the truck looks normal though, don't you think?"

"Hard to tell, from up here, in the dark." He looked at me. "But I'm gonna be keeping my eyes peeled watching all those trucks now, doncha know."

If there was something different, Minnesota Mike was sure to figure it out. I saw him looking at his watch.

"Hey now," he said, "I told yer folks I wouldn't keep you out too late and it's pert near midnight."

"Wow! Well, this sure beats having the girls pester me all evening. But I guess we better get on home."

"What're those gals up to anyways?" Mike checked over his seat belts, then pushed the clutch in and shifted the car into gear. I knew I better hang on. We were in for another fast take-off.

"They're sleeping outside in the tower to watch for the ghost lights!" I couldn't help it, but I burst out laughing.

Minnesota Mike joined me, only he seemed to think it was even funnier than I did. "Boy you're gonna love the great idear I jist got me." And we roared off toward home.

Chapter 21

Millie

Paisley stared in the direction Millie pointed. She turned, eyes wide, back to her friend as the two huddled together, the colorful lights dancing and bobbing above their heads.

"The ghost lights!" Paisley yelled and Millie clamped a hand over her mouth.

"Shush! You might make them go away."

"Oh, can the lights hear me?" Paisley burst out laughing.

"No, you dope, but you'll wake my parents."

"What's so bad about that? You don't want them to see the lights?"

Millie watched the lights continue to bob around. "I don't know," she whispered. "I want to figure this out for myself."

"Oh, that's right. We're supposed to be solving the hundred-year-old mystery about the ghost lights in the desert."

"Look!" Millie stared at her friend. "Are you with me in this mystery solving business or not? Maybe you think it's all a joke."

Paisley stood and motioned Millie to do the same. "I'm sorry, sometimes I make jokes that aren't that funny." She hugged her friend. "Yes, I'm with you."

Millie joined Paisley in the corner of the tower holding on to the rail and kept her eyes focused on the colored lights.

"They don't seem to be very far above us," Paisley said.

"You're right," Millie said. "So how would anyone else see them?"

"It's like they're shining just for us." Paisley took hold of Millie's arm, squeezing hard with both hands. "This is creepy."

"How creepy is it?" A deep voice sounded from below the tower.

Millie stifled a scream and wished now they had awakened her parents. "Someone is down there," she whispered.

Paisley's only response was whimpering.

Ready to scream for her parents, she waited to see what would happen next. They heard the voice again, closer this time, from on the ladder. The tone different, a high-pitched sound. "Oh, Millie, it's so creepy."

The lights stopped and a familiar belly laugh echoed from the back side of the house, joined by Jeremiah's loud laughter as his head popped up over the railing of the tower. He balanced on the ladder, laughing at the girls.

"I oughta push you off that ladder, Jeremiah Anderson!" Millie shouted. Now she was the one yelling and didn't care if her parents woke up.

"That was a mean trick," Paisley said.

"Oh, come on, little gals," Minnesota Mike's voice called from down below. "Doncha know, we was jist having some fun." He turned the colored spotlights back on and shined them up in the sky again. "I couldn't resist buying these at the discount store the other day after all the talk about the ghost lights."

"You've been hearing the stories, too?" Millie called down to him.

"Shore enough have, little missy."

"What have you heard?"

Minnesota Mike tipped his head down and rubbed the back of his neck. He looked back up at her. "Well now, this ain't the best way to carry on a conversation. Let's talk in the morning."

Jeremiah backed down the ladder and joined Mike on the ground. Minnesota put his arm around Jeremiah's shoulders. "I was a little late gittin' this here feller home, so I got to be going."

"Okay," Millie said. "Well I want to hear everything you know about the lights first thing tomorrow."

"Well, now, let's make a deal." Minnesota chuckled as he looked up at her. "I'll trade you my light story for you telling me about almost gittin' handcuffed."

Chapter 22

Jeremiah

I saw the first signs of daylight out my window, but I wasn't in any hurry to get out of bed. Millie was probably camped out in the hallway by my bedroom door waiting to pounce on me for spilling the beans to Minnesota Mike about her troubles the other day. Honestly, I hadn't meant to tell him. That old codger tricked me into admitting it. I wonder if he really knew the whole story already? And if he did, how would he have known? There was a lot more to that guy than just a fun-loving old drifter.

I stared up at the ceiling, pondering what Saturday had in store for me. Hopefully Paisley and Millie were still sound asleep in the tower and not stalking me. A chuckle slipped out though as I pondered Millie's predicament. She always wants new information about the latest happenings, but she wouldn't want to give up any information to get it. Hmm, how would she find out what Minnesota had heard about the ghost lights? For that matter,

I'd kind of like to know too since he never told me anything about the lights.

The safest thing for me to do was get up and disappear before the girls woke up.

My dad must have had the same idea this morning. He was already at work in his shop when I got down there. Which was good, since I didn't have keys to get in. My plan was just to get away from the house before I had to face Millie.

"What's up, Jeremiah?" Dad shut off his band saw and pushed his safety glasses up on his head. "You're up mighty early."

"So are you." I laughed and rubbed my hands together. "It's cold in here."

"Flip on that heater, will you?" Dad said. "I was so eager to get back on this project I forgot to do that."

"Well, I thought it was best to get away from the house before the noisy girls took over the kitchen."

"Aha." Dad nodded. Not sure if that "aha" was for what I said or for the piece of steel he was studying.

"Girls talk a lot, Dad." I held my hands close to the warm air flowing from the electric heater. "I mean a lot!"

"Don't I know it." Dad laughed. "Why do you think I love the shop?"

"Are you kidding me?" I never thought about a dad wanting to get away from so much talking.

"Yeah, just don't tell your mother."

"I'm sure she already knows."

He really laughed at that. "I'm pretty sure you're right."

Our conversation was interrupted by a knock on the door. That was unusual for this early. I looked over at Dad, but before he said anything the door opened.

"Well, how are you doing, Griffin?" Dad crossed the room quickly, his hand out to shake with Deputy Black. We hadn't seen him in several weeks. He'd been away on a special assignment.

"Max!" Deputy Black said, "It's great to see you, and you too, Jeremiah. I thought this might be too early, but looks like you're a couple of early birds."

I shook his hand, but looked at the other man who had followed him into Dad's shop. I'd never seen him before. He was in some kind of cop uniform, not riding gear like Deputy Black. It didn't look like the uniform Deputy Black wore on duty. A little different.

"I didn't hear you pull up, with the door closed and the heater running." Dad said. "Must be a little chilly riding this early."

"Boy, you can say that again," the other man said.
"Max, Jeremiah, this is my friend, Leon."

We all shook hands. "Are you a deputy, too?" I asked, thinking about the fake cop we had encountered earlier this week. I still had much to learn about this area we moved to.

"Border Patrol." Leon smiled at me. Friendly guy.

"That's why you look familiar," Dad said. "Were you working the checkpoint a few days ago?"

"Sure was."

"I think I chatted with you there."

"You may have at that," Leon said.

"Hey, can I ask you a question I've been wondering about?" This was my chance to find out why every time we went grocery shopping we had to sit and wait in a border check line on the way home.

"Sure, what's on your mind?"

"How come there's a border check when we're probably 20 miles from the border?"

"Actually, it's 54.4 miles from the border." Leon and Deputy Black chuckled. "But it's a good question."

Leon was the one to answer. "Things slip through the border and we're a secondary checkpoint they have to get through. You'd be surprised how much criminal activity gets discovered there."

"So you fellows got the day off?" Dad asked.

"Well, yes and no," Deputy Black said. "I've got the day off, so I told Leon I'd ride along with him on his patrol since he's doing it by quad today. I never pass up a chance to go riding."

"Do you think there are illegals crossing the border around here?" I felt like Millie, but I couldn't resist a few questions.

"Jeremiah." One look from Dad and I knew I overstepped the bounds.

"It's okay, Max," Deputy Black said. "We know your kids have a history of crime fighting, so it's not surprising the curiosity."

"We haven't spotted anything in this area recently," Leon said. "But we're always checking. Do you ride much off the property?"

"Sure, my sister and I go out just about every morning for a couple hours before we start our schoolwork."

He turned to head out the door. "Well, if you ever see any activity that seems suspicious, be sure to let us know."

I nodded my head but didn't speak. Why did I feel so guilty?

Chapter 23

Millie

Millie pulled the sleeping bag over her head to block out the creeping daylight. She made it a habit never to get up too early on Saturday, and especially sleeping outside, she didn't want to leave the warmth of the bag too soon.

"Millie, you awake?"

Paisley's whisper sounded muffled through the sleeping bag. What was she doing awake so early? Millie wondered.

"No."

Paisley pushed her shoulder. "I thought you wanted to get up early to track down Jeremiah."

Millie threw off her sleeping bag and sat straight up. "That's right! That rat! He told Minnesota Mike about me almost getting arrested." She looked over at Paisley, already dressed and rolling up her sleeping bag. "I wouldn't be surprised if my parents don't already know."

"Well, let's get going," Paisley said. "He's probably still asleep and you can sit outside his bedroom door so he can't hide from you."

"Good idea." Millie grabbed her sleeping bag and backpack and followed her friend down the ladder.

The smell of cinnamon rolls drew the girls to the kitchen before they could hunt down Jeremiah.

Millie's mom appeared to be the only person awake. "Oh good, we get first pick of the cinnamon rolls," Millie said as she took two from the center. She licked her fingers and poured a cup of milk before carrying her plate over to the table. "Glad we're the first ones up this morning, Mom. I love cinnamon rolls!" Paisley followed her to the table, also with two rolls.

"Well, you're the first ones to get the cinnamon rolls, but you're not the first ones up." Her mom joined them at the table with a glass of tea and piece of toast.

Millie dropped the roll back on her plate. "What do you mean?"

"Your dad and Jeremiah have been out of the house for at least an hour."

"Where did they go?" Millie did her best to sound nonchalant. She didn't want to alert her mom to how upset she was with Jeremiah.

"Well, they're most likely at the shop." Mom took a sip of her tea. "Your dad was up early to get back to the project he was working on. I saw Jeremiah head down that way shortly after your dad left the house."

Paisley and Millie exchanged a knowing glance. Her mom didn't miss that. "Why, what's up?" she asked. "Did you need to talk to one of them?"

Millie was already standing, gulping down her milk. She motioned to Paisley. "Come on, we can finish our cinnamon rolls while we walk."

"Millie?" Mom asked.

"Oh, nothing's up, I just want to let Jeremiah know I got first pick of the fresh cinnamon rolls," she said as the girls rushed out the back door.

"A likely story!" Paisley whispered once the door shut. The girls snickered as they rushed away from the house.

"Shush," Millie said. "My mom's already like a super sleuth. I'm sure she knows it's something more than the cinnamon rolls on my mind."

"Gee, maybe it runs in the family, ya think?" Paisley said.

But Millie wasn't listening. Her attention was fixed on the action down the road at the shop.

Who were those people? And what were they doing here so early? Didn't anyone sleep in on Saturdays?

Chapter 24

Jeremiah

I've heard the phrase "between a rock and a hard spot" before, but never understood what it meant. Until now.

Standing outside with my dad, we watched as Deputy Black and his friend Leon started their quads and waved goodbye. At the sound of their throttles accelerating, movement on the trail leading to the shop caught my eye. Oh no. It was Millie and Paisley headed right for me.

I had nowhere to go. Back into the shop to have my dad question why I looked sick when Leon said to watch out for suspicious activity or stay outside and get hammered by my sister for spilling the beans about the handcuffs?

This keeping secrets stuff was for the birds.

Now Millie was running and waving her arms like a wild woman. "Deputy Black!" I could hear her shouting his name over and over.

This might be my perfect opportunity to escape. Maybe it was my lucky day after all. Deputy Black must have glanced up toward the house before he headed to the gate, because now he and Leon were riding their quads in Millie's direction.

"Hey Dad, I'm going to head up and get some of those cinnamon rolls I saw Mom baking." Was my dad staring at me or was it my imagination? I wasn't waiting around to find out. "I'm starving!" I called over my shoulder as I took off in a slow jog toward the house.

As I got close to them, Millie was suffocating the deputy in a bear hug. Good thing for him he had a chest protector on. I thought I could jog right on past them undetected.

No such luck! "Where are you going, Jeremiah? I need to talk to you." She let go of the deputy and turned toward me.

"Hey, I'm starved." I kept heading toward the house. "Besides you need to visit with Deputy Black and meet his friend."

I'm sure I could hear the deputy laughing under his helmet. Maybe he had a sister once, too.

"Jeremiah, you're not getting off that easy!" I tried to ignore the sound of her annoying voice. Paisley hadn't caught up with Millie. She stood in the trail, looking a little tired, but I couldn't risk getting stuck talking to either of the girls. This might have been a trick. I waved and jogged right past her. Right now the cinnamon rolls were calling my name.

CHAPTER 25

Millie

Millie shoved the last of her breakfast in her mouth and took off in a run once she recognized the #37 quad down by the shop. She hadn't seen their friend in several weeks.

"Deputy Black!" she yelled and waved her arms as she ran. "Deputy Black!"

"Millie, you're going to wake up the entire neighborhood," Paisley said breathlessly as she ran along next to her.

Millie gave her a strange look. "What neighborhood? All three people who live on this dirt road? Deputy Black!"

"He sees you," Paisley said. She slowed to a walk. "You can stop screaming."

"I'm not screaming. I'm talking in a loud voice."

"Oh, brother." Paisley took a deep breath. "Wow, I'm out of shape, if that bit of running left me panting." Millie watched as her friend stopped, and leaned over with her hands propped on her knees.

"Are you okay?"

"Yeah, you go on ahead," Paisley said. "I'll catch up."

Millie resumed running even though she saw the deputy and his friend heading towards them on their quads.

She nearly attacked him with her enthusiasm as she threw her arms around his neck while he still sat on his quad. She heard the other man laughing.

"Millie, it's good to see you," he said.

"Deputy Black, we've missed you!"

He reached over and patted her shoulder. "You and your brother should start calling me Griffin. Deputy Black sounds so formal."

"Griffin?" Millie looked surprised. "Why would we call you something like that?"

He looked over at his friend and they both laughed. "Well, because it's my name. Is that a good enough reason?"

Millie felt herself blushing. "Oh, I'm sorry." An escaping giggle made her apology seem less than sincere. "I never heard a name like that before."

"Well, I'm happy to be the only Griffin you know."

Paisley caught up with them while they talked. "You remember Paisley, don't you?"

"Of course, she's the one who gives me free popsicles in the summer." Griffin smiled at Paisley. "Does your dad know you're cheating the store out of $2 every time I come in?"

Paisley's laugh sounded weak. "It was his idea," she said, her voice just above a whisper.

"Boy you are out of shape," Millie turned to her friend. "We didn't even run that far."

Paisley nodded, then collapsed in the dirt.

Chapter 26

Jeremiah

I couldn't believe we were in the waiting area of the emergency room again. It was only a few months ago we had been here for Minnesota Mike.

Millie sat next to me sniffing while our parents stood across the room talking in low voices to Deputy Black. Millie definitely wasn't her usual self, or she would have been pacing the floor trying to get close enough to hear what they said.

We both stood when the door from the emergency room opened. Paisley's mom approached our parents.

"Oh, thank God!" I heard my mom say. Mrs. Morgan smiled in our direction and motioned for us.

"Paisley would like to see you, Millie." She hugged my sister, who continued to cry.

"It will be okay." Mom patted Millie on the shoulder. She handed her some tissues before Millie followed Mrs. Morgan through the door.

"Oh, Max," Mom said, tears falling down her cheeks. Who could figure adults? Why would she tell Millie everything was okay, but cry as soon as Millie left? Dad was comforting her when Deputy Black put his arm around me and headed toward the door, dragging me along. "I'm thirsty." He smiled at me. "How about you?"

Deputy Black, okay, Griffin. I felt weird calling him by his first name, but he insisted. I have to admit it was easier than using his formal title. Anyway, Griffin prayed for the table full of food and I bit into the cheeseburger in front of me. I guess we were more than thirsty because a big plate of food sat in front of him, too.

As delicious as the cheeseburger tasted, it was hard to enjoy wondering what was going on downstairs in the emergency room. I kept waiting for Deputy, I mean, Griffin, to tell me what was happening with Paisley, but he just munched on his food. Maybe he was waiting for me to ask. I wished Millie was here. She would have asked a dozen questions by now.

He finished the last bite of his sandwich, wadded his napkin and dropped it on the plate, then looked at me. "Are you wondering what's going on with Paisley?"

I nodded. I'm not one to cry about everything, but I wasn't sure I could talk over the lump in my throat. I'd never had a friend get sick enough to go to the hospital before. And the worst part was seeing my mom cry.

"The good news is," Griffin smiled. "She is getting good care right now."

"But what is wrong with her?"

"Well, they will run tests to find out what it is."

"Maybe she got dehydrated," I said, "like when Minnesota Mike passed out and hit his head."

Griffin nodded. "I'm sure they're checking on that." His smile faded.

I could tell he had more to say, but I wasn't sure I wanted to hear whatever it was.

He reached across the table and patted my hand. "Remember what your parents have taught you."

He confused me. What did my parents teachings have to do with Paisley lying in an emergency room bed? “What’s that?” I asked.

“Trust God in all things.”

I took a deep breath. He definitely knew something.

CHAPTER 27

Millie

Millie followed Paisley's mom past the rows of curtained off beds. It reminded her of the time Minnesota Mike went to the emergency room. But this was worse. Paisley was just a kid. She shouldn't be having serious health problems. Millie wiped her eyes as a nurse pulled back the curtain near the end of the room.

There was Paisley. Even though she was hooked up to tubes and machines, she still had her usual big smile. Millie struggled to return the smile. "Did you bring your backpack?" Paisley asked.

"My backpack? Why in the world would you ask me that?"

Paisley smiled. "You always have everything in there we need."

"Oh." Millie looked around the little cubicle, listening to the beeps of the machines, watching the numbers bounce and change. Then she turned her attention back to Paisley. "Well, what do you need? I can check when I get home."

"A new heart."

Millie felt her own heart skip a beat. Was Paisley kidding? How could she sit there so calmly, even smiling, and say she needs a new heart? Millie's eyes went wide, and she looked from Paisley to her mother to the nurse. She wasn't often speechless. But right now, she had no idea what to say.

The nurse put her palm on Paisley's forehead, then smoothed her hair back. "Now Paisley, no one said anything about your heart." Millie heard Paisley's mother inhale deeply, but she kept her eyes on her friend.

She finally found her voice.

"What does she mean, Mrs. Morgan?" she whispered.

Paisley's mother didn't respond.

"It's common for patients to be hooked up to a heart monitor in the emergency room." The nurse reached over and took Millie's hand. "But that certainly doesn't mean she needs a new heart."

Paisley looked around the cubicle at the three of them, still smiling. "Well, I thought it was good for a little joke."

Millie grabbed Paisley's foot through the bedsheet. "Don't do that! You scared me!"

When her friend giggled, Millie felt herself relaxing.

"In fact, I think I get to go home soon. Isn't that right, Julia?"

The nurse's smile seemed forced. "Well, that's a possibility."

"I thought the doctor on duty said if she continues to be stable, it would be okay for her to leave later today." Mrs. Morgan looked over at Nurse Julia. "Or did I misunderstand him?"

Julia stared at the laptop on the bedside table, intently studying the information on the screen. Her breathing seemed heavy and Millie wondered if she was having health problems of her own. She finally looked over at Mrs. Morgan. "You didn't misunderstand him, but I'm hoping we can run a few more tests."

"Did the doctor order more tests?" Paisley said. It surprised Millie. Paisley rarely spoke up. Maybe she had been spending too much time with Millie. She stifled a chuckle at the thought.

"No, Paisley," Julia looked at the girl in the bed. "No, he didn't."

Chapter 28

Jeremiah

"On the surface, it appears Paisley is okay. Tests aren't showing any reason for her shortness of breath and fainting," Griffin said.

"I thought you told me her heart was racing after she fell."

"When I checked her pulse after she collapsed it was faster than the normal rate."

"Does that mean there is something wrong with her heart?" I asked.

"The doctor doesn't believe so. He feels it could be exertion from running in cold weather." Griffin looked away. He stopped talking, but it looked like a million thoughts were running through his head.

"Well, what are they doing for her, then? How are they going to figure out why this happened?"

"That's just the thing." Griffin looked back at me. "Sometimes there are no definite answers right away with health issues."

"Well, the tests should tell them something, right?"

"That would be nice if they did, but the tests they've run so far are showing nothing abnormal."

"Is that why my mom was so happy when Mrs. Morgan came out with the news?"

"I imagine so."

"Why did she cry then after Millie went back there?" This was so confusing. It's like he was saying she was all right, but maybe she wasn't all right.

"My guess would be she was holding back the tears while she was with Millie, and then, even though she was relieved, she was still scared."

"Huh?" If you're relieved, how can you be scared? I wished I could just go back to this morning when my biggest worry was my sister griping at me.

Griffin piled all the trash on our tray. "Emotions are complicated," he said. "Let's get back to the waiting room and see what's happening."

I followed him to the trash container and dropped everything in but my drink. That I wanted a refill on. As I watched the bubbling soda fill the cup, I remembered something Griffin said earlier.

"Hey," I said as we headed for the elevator. "Why did you say it would be important to remember to trust God?"

He smiled. "That's always important."

"Yeah, but it was like you knew something. Something bad."

Griffin pushed the call button next to the elevator and didn't look over at me. "Oh, is that what it sounded like?"

Chapter 29

Millie

"Why are you saying it like that?" Millie looked at the nurse. She was thankful her mom wasn't nearby to tell her it wasn't her place to ask questions. She held her breath, waiting to see if Mrs. Morgan would correct her. But the room was silent. Both Paisley and Mrs. Morgan also looked at the nurse. Maybe they wanted to hear the answer too.

"Well," Julia said. "Professionally, I'm not the one to order tests or make recommendations." Her voice trailed off.

"But?" Millie asked, probably more forcefully than she should have. She had to know. She knew something was going on. This nurse knew more than she was saying. And for whatever reason, neither Paisley nor her mom were asking any more questions.

"Millie," Mrs. Morgan said. "Let's wait for the doctor."

"Is Jeremiah here, too?" Paisley asked. She was like that, wanting to keep everyone calm. She probably figured changing the subject would help.

"Yes, he's with my parents and Deputy Black," Millie said, not happy about the new direction the conversation took. She wanted information, and she wanted it now.

Nurse Julia looked up and smiled. "Are you talking about Griffin Black?"

Shocked, Millie said, "Yes, do you know him?"

"I sure do, he's been friends with my husband and I for many years, but I haven't seen him in a long time. He used to work in this area, but once they transferred him we haven't crossed paths much."

"That's how we know him," Millie said. "He's the deputy where we live."

"I'm sure he loves it out there, especially being able to ride his quad whenever he's not on duty." She looked over at Paisley. "How are you feeling right now?"

"I feel good. Do you want to go out and say hi to him?"

"We're fine," Mrs. Morgan said. "We'll be okay waiting here until the doctor gets back to discuss discharge."

Millie saw a flicker of something in Julia's eyes. But the nurse smiled. "I'll check back with you in just a few minutes."

Determined to find out what the nurse really thought about Paisley's situation, Millie said, "I'll go along with her and let Jeremiah know how you're doing, Paisley."

Millie wasted no time digging for information as she walked beside the nurse. "So how did you meet Deputy Black?"

"Oh," Julia said as they headed toward the door to the waiting room. "We had an emergency at our home many years ago and Griffin was the first officer to respond."

"An emergency?" Millie probed.

"Yes, and we've been friends ever since." Julia pushed security buttons to unlock the waiting room door and Millie knew her window of opportunity to get more info was over.

Chapter 30

Jeremiah

"Julia!" Griffin crossed the waiting room floor in three giant steps. My parents looked as surprised as I did to see Deputy Black and a nurse hugging and laughing together.

"It's been so long since I've seen you," the nurse said.

I looked at Millie for answers. She stepped over near me. "This is Paisley's nurse, and she knows Deputy Black."

"He said to call him Griffin," I reminded her.

"It's hard to get used to that."

"But it's a lot quicker to say."

Griffin released Julia and turned toward our parents. "Max, Norah, this is my good friend Julia."

While the four of them exchanged greetings, Millie grabbed hold of my sleeve and led me across the waiting room. "Something is going on," she whispered.

She probably expected me to scold her for finding a mystery everywhere we went, but this time I agreed. "I'm thinking the same thing."

Her eyes grew big. "Why do you say that? You weren't even in the room."

"I can't figure it out for sure, but Griffin is acting strange about what's wrong with Paisley. What is the diagnosis?"

"I feel the same way about the nurse. She says the tests don't show anything, and Mrs. Morgan is even saying the doctor's talking about Paisley going home soon."

"So why do you think something is wrong?"

"It's the way the nurse acts. She kept staring at Paisley's info on the laptop, and she acted funny when Mrs. Morgan said something about Paisley going home. She wants them to run more tests."

"So are they going to?"

"That's just it, she said the doctor didn't order more tests."

"Well, how is Paisley?"

"She seems okay, smiling as usual. She wants to go home."

"Maybe the nurse is extra cautious." I looked up as Griffin motioned for us to join them.

He moved in between Millie and I and put his arms around our shoulders. "Julia, meet my good friends, Millie and Jeremiah."

"Well, Millie, I've met. In a manner of speaking," Julia said. "She's got a good head on her shoulders."

"Oh dear," our mom said. "Was she being too outspoken?"

I couldn't hold back a chuckle as Millie tensed up. Julia smiled. "No, she's inquisitive. I like that."

The nurse shook my hand. "I'm very glad to meet both of you."

She turned toward the door leading to the emergency room, then looked back. "I need to get back now, but I hope we can all get together sometime. I'm sure my husband would love to see Griffin again."

Griffin looked serious. "Let's do that and include Paisley's family. Then you can talk to them when you're off duty."

Julia dipped her head, looking at the floor, then reached into her pocket. When she made eye contact with him again, she wiped her eyes with a tissue. "No, Griffin. I can't. Will you talk to them, please?"

Chapter 31

Millie

Millie made it through the door before it shut by nearly walking on the heels of Julia. When the nurse turned, she was still wiping her eyes. “I’m sorry,” Millie said. “I know I didn’t ask, but I wanted to see Paisley once more before we leave.”

Julia sniffed and tucked her tissue back in her pocket. “It’s fine, Millie. I’m sure Paisley would like that.”

“Millie!” Paisley said. “I’m glad you came back. Mom said you were leaving so my dad can come and get us.”

“Oh, no! That must mean we will be taking care of the little boys.”

The girls laughed together.

“Millie,” Mrs. Morgan said, “you’ll only have Caleb. Donovan is coming with Paisley’s dad to pick us up. But you know the boys aren’t that difficult.”

"I know. But sometimes it's just fun to complain. How was their sleepover last night?"

"Well, I'm afraid there wasn't much sleeping until late in the night, which is why they weren't awake when we got the call this morning."

"That was nice of Mr. Morgan to keep Caleb so we could come to the hospital."

"He knew how much it would help Paisley having you and Jeremiah here." Mrs. Morgan smiled. "I'm so glad you two long lost best friends finally met each other."

Millie and Paisley laughed at her description. It was definitely the perfect way to explain their fast friendship.

"So, Millie, can you do something for me?" Paisley said.

"Sure, anything."

"Okay, go home and figure out what the source of the ghost lights are that people have been talking about." Paisley smiled at her friend.

"Are you kidding me? How can I even think about some silly ghost light legend when my best friend is lying in a hospital bed?"

"That's why I asked you to do it. I don't want you worrying about me. You might as well be finding things out to tell me until I can look for clues with you."

"I don't know how soon that will be, Paisley," Mrs. Morgan said.

"Mom, you said yourself the doctor found nothing wrong. You're not going to turn me into an invalid, are you?"

"Your mom is wise to want to keep a close eye on you for a few days," Julia joined in their conversation when she stepped back into the cubicle.

What does she know? Millie wondered. She was dying to tell Paisley what she heard Julia say to Griffin in the waiting room, but she didn't want to talk in front of Mrs. Morgan.

Paisley's mom lost her smile at Julia's words. Maybe she too sensed that Julia knew more than she was saying.

"So it will be important to keep her close by me for a few days?"

Julia blinked several times as if to hold back tears. "Yes," she said. "I think so."

Chapter 32

Jeremiah

The roar of Minnesota Mike's buggy broke the silence before I could see him. A trail of dust gave away his location out on the dirt road leading up to our property. I knew Caleb was loving his first ride. He'd been begging for one ever since Mike brought the buggy over to show the family. What a weekend this was for him. Last night his first sleepover with Paisley's little brother, Donovan, and now his first ride in a dune buggy.

I'll bet Mike would slide sideways into the gate, since he liked to see how long he could wait to hit the brakes before making the turn. I thought about walking down to watch, but knew I'd never get there in time.

I could hear the giggles over the sound of the engine as the buggy cruised up and skidded to a stop in front of the porch.

"Jeremiah!" Caleb shouted through his helmet. "That was so much fun!"

I'd never seen the boy so excited. What a welcome relief to see so much happiness. It was a big change from our day so far. Hopefully Paisley would be coming home soon, but for now, I just wanted to put that out of my mind and soak up the excitement of this little boy.

"You weren't scared at all?" I helped him out and unfastened his helmet.

"No sirree." Minnesota answered before Caleb could. Mike was already out of the driver's seat and coming around to the porch. "I'm telling you, he wanted me to go faster and faster." He reached over and tousled Caleb's already messed up hair. "I don't think there's a fearful bone in this feller's body."

Caleb reached up and grabbed hold of Minnesota Mike's hand, pulling it down and holding on to him. "I trust you," he looked up into Mike's eyes. "I know you wouldn't hurt me."

Minnesota knelt and hugged him. He looked about as happy as a man could be.

"Caleb! You're home." Mom stepped out the door and hurried down the porch steps to where Mike and Caleb were embracing. "Look at you, you're glowing!"

She looked over at Mike once he stood back up. "Thank you so much for bringing him home. This is the happiest I've ever seen him."

"Well, it was a little selfish of me," Mike said. Then lowered his voice as Mom hugged the boy. "I was hoping to get some word on Paisley."

"I'm starving, Miss Norah! Are there any cookies?"

Mom took hold of Caleb's hand. "I believe there are three cookies left with your name on them. Let's go find them." As they stepped up to the front door, Mom turned to me. "Jeremiah, can you tell Mike what we know?"

"Sure, Mom."

The excitement had gone from Minnesota's face, replaced by what was probably worry about Paisley. He must have been hiding it from Caleb.

"Well, there are two different versions about Paisley's condition," I said. "Which one do you want, the official hospital position, or mine and Millie's?"

“I want them both,” Minnesota said. He motioned me toward the driver’s side of his buggy, then stood with his back to the house. I followed.

“Before you fill me in,” he said. “There’s something I need to tell you.”

Chapter 33

Millie

"Mike!" Millie burst out the front door and down the porch steps into Mike's waiting arms. His long beard tickled her cheek as she hugged him. He squeezed her tight, then held her at arm's length. She swiped at tears. "We don't know what's wrong with Paisley."

"Jeremiah and I was jist talking about that special little lady." Millie saw a look pass between Mike and Jeremiah.

She turned to her brother. "What are you talking about that I don't know?"

"Millie, you know good and well I don't know any more than you know."

She looked back to Minnesota Mike. "I saw the look you gave each other. You were talking about something else."

Jeremiah took a deep breath. "Honestly, we barely got started when you burst on the scene like a whirlwind."

"Well, now, little lady, you are just enough of a little detective that you pick up on ever last little thing," Minnesota said.

"You lost me there, Mike," Jeremiah said. Millie saw Jeremiah stare at the older man and realized he must have been telling her the truth.

"Well, we was gittin' ready to talk about Paisley, but then I said first there was something I needed to talk about."

"Oh, that's right," Jeremiah said.

"And you don't want to talk about it in front of me, so that's why you were staring at each other like that," Millie accused.

"I'm still lost, Mil, because I wasn't staring at anyone. Haven't you heard about innocent until proven guilty?"

"Well, little lady, yer right, I did take a quick like glance over to your brother, because I wasn't sure I was ready to tell the both of you."

"So, I was right," Millie turned to her brother. "I told you. It's something you're hiding from me."

Jeremiah threw up his arms. "Okay, Millie, you're right. I'm hiding something from you. In fact, I'm hiding it so well, I'm hiding it from myself too, because I've said ten times I don't know what's going on."

"Hey, hey, what's all this yelling out here?"

Millie jumped at the sound of her dad's voice.

"I was trying to talk on the phone and couldn't hear over all the yelling."

Before either of them could respond to the reprimand, Mike intervened. "I'm sorry, Max, I think I've got them all worked up."

Their dad stepped down off the porch and shook Mike's hand. "Well, it's easy to do right now," he said. "We're all a little on edge with Paisley in the hospital."

"I feel real bad about that," Mike said.

"You were a big help to bring Caleb home, he sure was excited about getting to ride in your buggy."

Mike's smile vanished. "Well, that's what I was getting ready to talk to the kids about."

"What about Caleb?" Millie interrupted. "Is he all right?"

"Now, now, there's nothing wrong with that little tyke."

"Well, what is it then?" Millie pushed and heard her brother growl under his breath.

"Millie, give the man a chance to talk."

Someday, she would do that, she vowed. She would wait for people to get around to whatever it is they were trying to say, instead of butting in with so many questions. But today wasn't that day. "What's wrong with Caleb?" She pushed again when he still hadn't responded.

Mike stared off into the distant hills to the south of them. Then he looked over at their dad.

"It's what he said just as we was turning into your gate, that's got me concerned."

Chapter 34

Jeremiah

I stepped closer to my sister. I wanted to clamp my hand over her mouth but I just whispered, "Wait for him to finish!"

Millie glared at me, but I could tell she knew I was right. She surprised me when she did what I said. She didn't take kindly to orders. Especially from me.

"Go on," Dad said. "What did Caleb say?"

"Well, he pointed over to them hills in the distance." Mike motioned toward the hills. "There was a glare coming from there. Kinda like the sun hitting some shiny object. He got real excited, in fact I slowed down to a full stop 'cause I never seen the little feller so excited about something."

"So did he say something while he was pointing?" Millie asked. I thought about jabbing her in the side, but figured that would slow the story down. She would never change.

"Yep, he shore did. He said 'it's the light, let's go find Sissy.'" Mike looked at Dad, then over at me and my sister and shook his head. “I ain’t never heard him talk like that and I didn’t even know he had a sissy.”

“Did you ask him what he meant?” Dad said.

“Well, I tried,” Minnesota said. “I said something like, ‘Where is Sissy?’ and he jist kept saying ‘at the light, Sissy’s at the light.’”

“Then what happened?” It was my turn to throw out a question.

“I didn’t rightly know what to say to the little feller so’s I jist said, I gotta git you back to Max and Norah, they miss you something awful. We’ll check on Sissy some other time.”

“Was he okay with your response?” Dad asked.

“He was more than okay.” Minnesota Mike smiled. “His eyes lit up, and I knowed he was smiling under his helmet. He said, ‘Let’s go! Miss Norah’s probably got cookies!’ And no more talk about his sissy.”

“Dad,” I said, “did you ever ask Deputy Black if Caleb has a sister?”

Dad nodded his head. “Yes, as a matter of fact, we discussed Caleb’s mom today.”

Chapter 35

Millie

"What did he say, Dad?" Millie knew her question would annoy her brother, but her dad was taking too long to answer.

"He said he didn't know of a sister."

"Well, is he going to look into it? I mean, can't he get in touch with the mom and ask her?" She avoided looking at her brother as she fired off the questions.

"Yes. He said he'd try to visit her at the jail in the next few days."

"Good, then we can figure out what that kid's talking about," Millie said.

"Well, now, little missy, I wouldn't count on that too much." They all looked over at Mike's unexpected words.

"Why do you say that?" Jeremiah said.

"Well, could jist be my suspicious mind." He looked at their dad, smoothing his beard down as he turned his head in the other direction. Millie noticed he always fiddled with his beard like that when he had something on his mind.

"Well, you must have a reason," Millie prodded.

"Sometimes I jist git a feeling about people. And she don't seem too trustworthy to me."

The front door banged open and Caleb barreled down the steps, "Mike! You're still here!" Caleb threw his arms around the older man. "Can you take me out for another ride? Can you?"

Even Dad looked like he'd have a hard time saying no to the little guy. Mike was looking in Dad's direction, probably trying to figure out how to answer.

"Tell you what, Caleb. If Mike has time, he can take all three of you out for a short buggy ride."

"Now doncha know, that's jist what I was thinkin' on doin'." Mike nodded.

Any other time Millie would have been excited, especially since she was the only one who hadn't been in Mike's buggy yet. But now she just wanted to wait for Paisley to come home from the hospital.

"You kids go git your helmets on," Mike said, "and I got the best idea yet. We'll head back over to the lodge and see if'n Paisley has come home yet."

With that destination, Millie was fully on board with this change of plans. She and Jeremiah turned toward the house as their mom stepped through the open door.

"Max." She motioned for their dad. "A phone call for you."

Her dad continued to fasten Caleb's helmet. "I'll be right there," he called over his shoulder.

"It's urgent," Mom said. "Griffin says he needs to talk with you right away."

Chapter 36

Jeremiah

"So, Caleb, how's about we go hunt for yer sissy before we check on Paisley?" Minnesota Mike's voice was low, but I caught wind of what he was saying. I looked up to see Millie heading into the house.

"Hey, Millie, grab my helmet too." She'd kill me if she knew I was making her get my helmet so I could stay and hear this conversation. But I'd make it to up to her later. Or maybe I already made it up to her when I kept her from getting handcuffed the other day. I stepped over near the buggy. Mike was fastening the belts on Caleb's seat.

"Is the light still shining over there?" Caleb said. "Cause if the light ain't shining, she won't be there no more."

Minnesota looked up at me, and I shrugged. Who knows what this kid is talking about? But it was the same way the other night. When he saw bright lights shining in our direction, he started talking about a sister.

"No, sonny boy, there ain't no more light shining."

"Then we missed her again." Caleb grabbed hold of the straps on his safety harness with both hands. "I'm all ready to go!"

"Who did we miss?" Millie appeared next to me and shoved my helmet into my hands. I wasn't sure what to say. I didn't know if I should talk about it in front of Caleb.

"Jeremiah!" She jabbed my arm with her pointy index finger, then pulled her helmet down over her head. "What did I miss when I was waiting on you hand and foot?"

"What do you mean, waiting on me? You had to get your own helmet, anyway."

"Yeah, but you didn't tell me there was something interesting going on out here."

"You two stop yer jawing and git those helmets on so we can take off, afore your pops forgits he told us we could all go out." Minnesota Mike climbed into the driver's seat.

"Look, I'll tell you about it later." I could tell my sister was not happy about having to wait. "I promise," I said, fastening my helmet.

The buggy roared to life as Millie climbed in the seat behind Mike. I stepped up on the outside rail to get in behind Caleb, just as I heard Dad call out my name.

Millie must have heard him too. She tapped Mike on the shoulder, and he shut the engine off. Dad stepped around to the driver's side.

"That was Griffin." Dad looked serious. Maybe he learned something about this mysterious sister Caleb keeps talking about.

"He wants to talk to all of us later today."

"All of us?" Minnesota said. "That include me?"

"Yes," Dad said. "Yes, it does. And it includes Paisley's family too."

Well, it must have nothing to do with Caleb, I figured. "What's this about, Dad?"

Millie looked at me, probably startled that I asked a question before she did.

"He didn't say, just said it was important he talks with all of us as soon as possible. He already lined it up with Mr. Morgan. We'll meet at their house"

“Does that mean we don’t get to go for our ride?” Caleb tugged Mike’s arm. “Ask Mr. Max if we can still go for a ride.”

Dad smiled at Caleb. “Tell you what, why don’t you all go for your ride anyway and Mom and I will meet you over at Paisley’s house in about an hour.”

“Yippee!” Caleb howled, then squirmed in his seat trying to turn around. “Did you hear that, Millie?”

“I sure did.” Millie reached up and patted Caleb’s shoulder. “He said we get to go.”

“No, not that,” Caleb said. “He called Miss Norah my mom!”

Chapter 37

Millie

Caleb's words startled Millie. She thought he missed his own mother. Before she could dwell on the reasons for him being so excited about her mom, a shriek flew out of her mouth as Minnesota Mike floored the buggy. They took off so fast her head bounced back against the high back seat.

Millie hung on to the safety harnesses cinched over her chest and looked over at her brother as they flew along the bumpy road heading to the back of their property. Jeremiah held both thumbs up as he whooped and hollered.

She peered ahead to see if Mike would skirt around the drop-off she knew was ahead, but he kept the pedal to the floor and the steering wheel straight. She opened her eyes wider and looked over at her brother to see if it worried him, but she saw no such thing. His head jostled around and muffled laughter escaped from his helmet. Before she could worry much more, she felt the car sailing as they launched off the embankment.

Caleb's happy screeching from the seat in front reassured her this ride wasn't scaring him, not one bit. She tensed, waiting for the landing, but to her surprise it was softer than she expected. Must be that suspension she heard her dad raving about with Mike when he was checking out the buggy. She remembered all she cared about was the color.

Once off their property Mike headed the buggy in the direction of the old abandoned store. Millie was glad for the chance to pass by. She hoped she'd get another glimpse of the phony cop. But instead of following the road all the way to the store, Mike cut off in a sandy wash, speeding up and sliding the buggy right and left all to the thrill of Caleb who howled with excitement at every slide and bump.

Too soon their adventure ended, and they were cruising into the driveway of the Ridge Riders Lodge. Millie wanted to undo her helmet when she saw Paisley climbing out of the family car parked in front of the store entrance, but her dad had drilled safety into her. She waited until the buggy came to a full stop a few parking spaces away from her friend.

In record time she got her safety harnesses undone and leaped out, running over to embrace Paisley, helmet and all.

"Millie, it's so good to be home." Paisley's voice sounded muffled as she hugged Millie.

"Here, let me take this off, so I don't knock you out and send you back to the hospital." Both girls laughed as Millie stepped away. She slipped off her helmet, then smoothed her hair, eyes glued on her friend. It was so good to see her out of the hospital bed and back home.

"Hey, isn't that your parents pulling in over there?"

"Yeah," Millie said. "Didn't you know?"

Paisley's head jerked back toward Millie. "Know what?" Then she clapped her hands. "Is it a welcome home party for me?"

Millie's stomach flip-flopped when she realized her friend didn't know they were coming over to hear something Deputy Black wanted to tell them. She wasn't sure why, but she felt scared. And since Paisley hadn't been told anything, she felt especially scared for Paisley.

"Look!" Paisley's excitement grew. "It's Deputy Black! I bet this is a party! My mom couldn't wait for them to let me out of the hospital."

Millie forced a smile. The girls watched as Paisley's mom met Millie's parents at their car. "Maybe we should go see if they decorated." Millie said when she saw that Deputy Black wasn't alone.

It seemed best to distract Paisley. Even though Millie didn't know any details, she was sure it wasn't a party.

Especially when she saw Julia, the nurse, in the passenger seat of Deputy Black's car.

CHAPTER 38

Jeremiah

I didn't envy my sister right now. I watched as she tried to figure out how to respond to Paisley who had the mistaken idea we were all here for a welcome home party. The look on my sister's face when she saw Deputy Black drive into the parking lot with the nurse in the passenger seat matched how I felt.

Something wasn't right. I knew Griffin was acting strange in the hospital cafeteria.

"Dad!" I did one of those whisper-yells trying to catch his attention and crossed the parking lot in a couple big steps to catch him before he went in. "What's going on? Why are we all here?"

Dad's arm felt good around my shoulders as he led me away from the others. "I'm not sure, Jeremiah. But we'll find out soon."

"Why is the nurse here?"

"That's a surprise to me too. Griffin didn't say anything about bringing her. He just said he had some information about Paisley's health and her parents wanted our family to be here with them to hear it."

"Okay, that's weird." I shook my head. "We were all just at the hospital, why would a cop know more about Paisley's health than the doctor in the emergency room?" I inhaled deeply and watched as Griffin and Julia got out of his car.

Dad nodded. "You got me. I'm as confused as you are." He pointed back toward the car. "Let's go help Mom."

She had the back doors to the SUV open and looked like she was pulling out something bulky. Just as I was about to ask what she was doing, giant colorful balloons popped out of the back, bouncing around on ribbons my mom held.

"Those are beautiful, Norah!" Dad said. "I can't believe you came up with something like that on the spur of the moment."

"I told you that helium tank would come in handy one day," Mom said. "Jeremiah, will you get those presents? Max, can you carry the cake?"

"Mom, you're amazing." I reached in and grabbed a gift bag and two wrapped parcels. "Did you know Paisley thinks we're all over here for a welcome home party?"

Mom wiped tears from her eyes with her free hand. "I didn't, but God did." She reached out and hugged me. "I've been accumulating party things and gifts recently and I didn't even know why. But today God showed me what they were for."

Dad shoved the back doors shut with his elbow as he balanced the double layer chocolate cake with both hands.

"I didn't have time to write anything on the cake," Mom said.

"I don't think Paisley will mind," I said. "I sure don't. I can't wait to get a piece."

"Well, let's go get this party started," Dad said.

"And whatever happens at this party, God's got it all under control." Mom sounded confident, but was still wiping tears as she turned to follow Dad, the helium balloons bouncing all around her head.

Chapter 39

Millie

As much fun as the impromptu party was, Millie figured everyone, even Paisley, was relieved that the time had arrived to find out what this get-together was all about.

The room grew quiet. Even Caleb and Donovan stopped talking where they sat near the stairwell playing with cars. Or at least they had cars in their hands. Mostly they were watching the adults. Probably wondering, just like everyone else, what was happening.

Griffin scooted to the edge of his chair, his elbows propped on his knees as he leaned forward and surveyed the room. Julia sat in a folding chair a few feet from him, close to Paisley. She smiled in her direction and reached over and patted Paisley's shoulder. Millie was across the room next to her mother.

After Griffin looked around at each one of them, he took a deep breath. "I know this seems strange to all of you." Millie noticed that Julia dipped her head down and fidgeted with a tissue in her lap.

"Julia has some information that might be helpful. It may or may not apply to what happened with Paisley today. If it doesn't, that's wonderful, but if it does, it's important that we share this."

"Thank you," Paisley's dad said. "We appreciate it and we'd like to hear what you have to say."

"Julia is the one with the knowledge about the subject, but it's difficult for her." Griffin paused to look at Julia, but her head was still down. "We decided I would share the information and then if you have questions, she'll answer them."

"How come she didn't talk to us about this at the hospital?" Millie said.

"Millicent!" Both parents scolded her at once. She didn't look, but no doubt her brother was giving her a dirty look too. Someday maybe she'd learn to stop blurting out whatever she wanted.

"We will explain all of that, Millie." Julia's voice was kind. At least she didn't seem to mind Millie's curiosity getting the better of her all the time.

"I met Julia and her husband on a 9-1-1 call many years ago." Griffin took another deep breath and looked at Julia again. Her head was up. She nodded for him to continue.

"They found their infant son unresponsive in his crib. We could not resuscitate him."

Gasps were heard around the room.

"Why did that happen?" Paisley's soft voice asked what they all wondered.

"At the time it was referred to as Crib Death." Millie could see her parents nodding their heads like they were familiar with the term. "It was accepted as an unexplained death that sometimes occurs with infants."

"Do you know something now about what caused the baby's death?" Paisley's mom said.

"Yes." Griffin looked at Julia again before he continued. "About ten years ago, there was another sudden death in their family." His words hung heavy in the air.

Even Millie couldn't bring herself to ask who it was.

CHAPTER 40

Jeremiah

"Hey now, what do you all say, if I take these young'uns out for a little walk right about now?" Minnesota Mike's voice was a welcome interruption. I mean, where was Griffin heading with this story? Was he saying that Paisley might die? How did we go from worrying about ghost lights, fake cops and handcuffs to learning that one of our friends might die? This didn't seem real. I couldn't even bring myself to look at my sister.

Mike was already moving across the room toward Caleb and Donovan. The little boys gathered up their cars. They seemed more than willing to go with him. Hopefully, they didn't understand what Griffin was talking about.

"Thank you, Mike," Mrs. Morgan said. "I think that's a good idea."

Caleb stopped by my mom on his way out and gave her a hug. "I love you, Miss Norah," he whispered. I think the little squirt could tell she needed some comfort.

Mr. Morgan left the room then, too. He returned carrying a tray with a pitcher of ice water and empty glasses. The welcome break gave us all a chance to stand and stretch. We hadn't been sitting very long, but this conversation made it seem like we'd been talking for hours.

Once everyone sat back down, Julia surprised us by picking up where Griffin left off.

"It was my daughter." She smiled at Paisley. "She was your age."

Mrs. Morgan moved over to Julia and embraced her. "I'm so sorry." Paisley's mom looked like she was struggling not to break down.

"To make a long story short, we discovered that my husband and I carry a gene that causes problems with electrical impulses in the heart. We passed it on to our daughter, and we suspect to our son. It doesn't happen in every family that carries it, but there is the risk of sudden cardiac arrest if it isn't treated."

Mrs. Morgan covered her face with her hands and breathed a loud whisper, "Thank you, Jesus." Then she looked at Julia. "So this is treatable?"

"Yes," Julia nodded. "And if that is what caused our son to die and it had been discovered, we could have had our daughter tested and treated."

"Were there any symptoms?" my mom asked.

"Not that we recognized," Julia said. "She fainted a few times, and we took her in for testing, but no one connected it."

"Which explains why you want us to know about this?" Mr. Morgan said.

"Yes," Julia said. "I'm not allowed to make medical recommendations, which is why I couldn't discuss this at the hospital, but as one mother to another, I urge you to get her checked out by a pediatric cardiologist."

The door banged open suddenly. "My sissy! Can I go see my sissy, Miss Norah?" Caleb flew into the room like a whirlwind. "She's shining the light for me."

I don't know if it was right to feel like this, but it relieved me in a big way to have Caleb interrupt us. I was ready to get out of this room. Sorry Paisley.

"Come on, Caleb!" I grabbed the young boy by the hand and led him back out the door. "Let's go see where your sissy is."

Chapter 41

Millie

Millie watched longingly as her brother escaped the depressing conversation. She looked over at Paisley and saw that same desire in her eyes.

"So, can I say something?" Millie said to no one in particular.

"Well, that's a refreshing change, Millie." Her dad laughed.

"What do you mean?"

"You rarely ask, you just jump right in with both feet."

"Oh." Even though her dad was laughing, she wasn't sure it was okay to laugh yet.

"Yes, Millie, what did you want to ask?" Julia said.

"Well, it isn't really a question. And it's kind of off topic."

"That's okay," Mr. Morgan said. "I think we can all use a breather here."

"I didn't know nurses wore cowboy boots." The suede boots with the little bit of fringe had fascinated Millie the entire time she'd been listening to Griffin and Julia talk. Maybe it was her mind distracting her from the scary conversation.

Julia reached down and touched her boots while relieved laughter spread around the room. "Well, sure, when I'm not on duty, it's what I live in."

"Wow."

"Nurses are people too, Millie." Paisley smiled at her friend, then looked over at Julia. "I wouldn't mind having a pair just like that."

"Say, while we're moving on to new topics," Griffin said. "I'm sure Julia wouldn't mind if someone offered her a dune buggy ride while we're here visiting."

Millie saw Julia's face light up. "I would love that! I haven't been out cruising around in the desert since I was a kid."

"Really, Julia?" Millie said. "Did your parents have a buggy?"

"Millie!" Paisley laughed.

"I know, I know, Paisley," Millie said. "Nurses are people too."

"They sure did, Millie. I have so many wonderful memories. We used to stay at an RV park out here somewhere. I don't think I could even find it now."

"What was it called?" Griffin seemed surprised to learn about this side of Julia.

"The campground, I'm not sure, but it was right near a store called Ye Olde Dry Brook Trading Post. I loved that store!"

"That's the store!" Millie jumped up. "Jeremiah and I were there recently." Her eyes grew large as she looked over at Paisley. She had almost given away the trouble she'd gotten into there. She needed to get back there to figure out what was going on. How was Paisley going to help her with that now?

"So, it's still there?" Julia clapped her hands together and turned toward Griffin. "Can you take me by there on our way home? I wonder what time it closes."

"Well, the building is there," Millie said, "but the store is closed down."

Julia looked disappointed. "They had so many fun things to look at in that store. I'd save my money in between desert trips just to buy trinkets from the trading post whenever we came to the desert."

No one had noticed Minnesota Mike step back into the room, but he must have been there long enough to hear part of the conversation.

"Well, now that store's for sale, doncha know?"

"Oh, so maybe it will re-open soon?" Julia looked hopeful.

"It's been for sale for quite a few years," Mr. Morgan said.

Minnesota Mike pointed in Julia's direction. "But doncha know, if'n the right person were to come along and buy it, then it could open back up again."

Chapter 42

Jeremiah

I stirred the fire with my roasting stick, watching the charred remains of the marshmallow turn to black crust. After the last of the marshmallow dropped into the fire, I dropped the stick onto the edge of the firepit and leaned back in my chair. It felt so good to sit out here, staring up into the stars. What a day this had been.

"Hey, maybe we'll see the ghost lights while we're out here tonight."

I looked over at my sister when she spoke. She was doing the same thing I was, gazing up into the dark sky.

"You don't give up on this mystery solving business, do you?" I said.

"Why should I?"

"Well, look what's going on with Paisley."

"Even Paisley told me to watch for them."

"Are you kidding me? Isn't she scared?" I hadn't talked with Paisley after we heard Julia's story today, but when Minnesota

Mike and Griffin took Julia out in the buggy, I saw Millie and Paisley sitting on one of the outdoor benches talking.

"I'm not kidding you and no she isn't scared."

"Would you be if you heard you might have something you could die from?" I sat up in my chair and stared at my sister. I'm not sure I understood girls.

"Well, I don't think we can really know if something would scare us until we're experiencing it for ourselves," Millie said.

That made a lot more sense than I would have expected my sister to make. It's easy to say how we think we would handle something, but she's right, we don't really know.

Millie continued. "Paisley said they don't even know if she has the same thing Julia's kids had and even if she does, Julia said there is treatment. She said maybe it's a good thing she fainted today."

"Wow." I nodded my head. "I'd like to think I could have that much faith not to worry about health problems."

"Why focus on health problems when there are more fun things to focus on?" Millie said.

"Like ghost lights, no doubt?"

"Yes, and speaking of lights, look over in that direction." Millie stood and stared toward the dirt road.

"I don't see any light," I said.

"No, but listen. It's like the other night. We hear the loud rumble of a truck, but don't see any truck lights."

"Well, what's that have to do with ghost lights?"

"Maybe nothing, but it sure is strange. We've heard that three times now."

"That reminds me," I said. "I never told you what Minnesota Mike and I saw the other day when we drove by the trading post."

Millie jerked her head in my direction. "What?" she demanded. "And why didn't you tell me?"

"Because you would have ridden right back to the store and got arrested for real this time."

"You can't get arrested by a fake cop."

"Really? Well, he was doing a good job of starting to arrest you the other day."

My sister shivered. "Don't remind me."

The front door opened, and Dad wandered over to the firepit. "It's been quite a day, hasn't it?" he settled in a chair. I saw Millie slump down in her chair. I knew what she was thinking. She wouldn't get to hear about the trading post now that Dad was out here.

"Yeah, sure has," I said. "That's the last thing I ever expected to hear Griffin telling us."

"Paisley's parents are handling it well," Dad said. "They see it as a blessing to have the chance to get her tested. They're grateful the incident today wasn't more serious."

"Paisley doesn't want to dwell on it," Millie said. "At least, that's what she told me."

"Yeah, she just wants to get back to solving mysteries with Millie." I said.

Dad smiled. "Well, that's probably a good way to deal with it. Wait for the tests and in the meantime focus on other things."

"That reminds me of something I've been wanting to ask you." Millie turned toward Dad. "Paisley and I read in a book that the old store closed down because one of the partners died. Was he murdered?"

I couldn't hold my laughter back. "You and your mysterious stories." Millie gave me a dirty look and turned back to Dad.

"Sorry to burst your bubble, Millie." Dad smiled. "It wasn't murder, but it was tragic. He fell from the roof while doing some repairs. His partner was grief-stricken at losing his best friend and just locked up the store one day and left."

"Oh, that's pretty sad. Well, at least I can tell Paisley I solved one mystery."

Dad reached into the marshmallow bag and poked one onto the end of the stick I left on the fire ring. "Speaking of mysteries," he said, as he held it over the flames. "What did you find out from Caleb about his sissy shining a light?"

Chapter 43

Millie

Millie sat straight up in her chair at this new topic. She didn't mind waiting to hear what happened at the trading post if she could finally learn something about Caleb's mysterious sister.

Jeremiah leaned forward in his chair. "Well, when I got outside, Caleb was staring toward the mountains south of us. You can see them better from Paisley's house."

"Did you see a light shining?" Millie said, and then cringed, expecting Jeremiah to get annoyed.

"No, so I asked him where the light was. He shrugged his shoulders and said it went away again."

"What about Mike?" their dad asked. "Did he say if he saw the light?"

"I didn't ask him." Jeremiah said. "But I asked Caleb why he thinks that is his sister."

“And?” Millie said. He didn’t have to drag this out and keep them in suspense. She wished she had been out there with Caleb, but she knew she did the right thing by staying inside with Paisley.

“He said he hasn’t seen her in a long time. That she went away when he was a little boy. Before she left, she told him she would shine a light for him.”

“Well, how does he know it’s that light? Did he say where she went?”

“Millie, I didn’t ask him a thousand questions like you would have.”

“That’s probably best,” their dad said. “It may be his imagination. We don’t even know if he has a sister.”

“Has he mentioned it since we’ve been home?”

“I haven’t heard him say anything, Millie.” Their dad popped his roasted marshmallow into his mouth, stood and stretched his arms over his head. “This has been a long day, we should all get some sleep, so we’re refreshed and ready for church in the morning.”

Millie looked at her brother, but neither of them moved as their dad turned toward the house. “Can we have 30 more minutes, Dad?”

“Make it 15, Millie,” Dad said, “I’ll have Mom let you know when it’s time.”

Millie waited until the front door latched shut. “Okay, now tell me what you saw at the store and it better be more useful than the lame info you had about Caleb’s sister.”

“Well, it’s kind of hard to have news about someone who probably doesn’t even exist,” her brother said. “And don’t be so bossy about it.”

Millie watched as he stood and stared into the darkness. She was tempted to push him for info, but their dad was right. This had been a long day, and her brother was edgy. She’d get no information from him if she made him mad. Being patient seemed wiser than risking him turning and heading into the house.

“It’s nothing big,” he said. “The other day when Mike and I were picking up his buggy, he drove me down Monument Road.”

“Why?”

“Millie!”

"Okay, okay, no more questions. I'll be satisfied with whatever you tell me."

"He wanted to check out the area where he's heard people talking about the ghost lights. But when we went past the old store, I saw that guy, you know, the fake cop. He stared right at me, even pointed his finger at me threateningly."

"He recognized you?"

"Yeah, but that's not all," Jeremiah said. "There were other people there, probably two or three others and several kids. They were heading into the store. Even Mike seemed to think it was strange."

"Do you think they want to buy it? Maybe a realtor was showing it to them?"

"That's what I said to Mike, but he said no one should be there. He seemed to know something about the place."

"Mike seems to know stuff about a lot of things."

"Yeah, like how did he know about the man trying to handcuff you?"

"I thought you told him. I've been mad at you ever since."

"Then why have you been talking to me?" Jeremiah snickered.

"Well, in all the confusion with Paisley I forgot I was mad," Millie said. "But now I remember."

"No, I didn't tell him. Well, part of it slipped out, and I tried to stop it, but then he seemed to know anyway, maybe not the whole story, but some of it."

"I guess if I want to find out what he knows about the ghost lights, I'll have to give in and tell him the story."

"Tell who what story?" their mom said.

"Mom!" Millie jumped, almost tipping her chair over. "You scared me, I didn't hear you come out."

"I've been calling you two, but you're so engrossed in your conversation, you didn't hear me."

Millie looked at her brother and he shrugged. "I never heard anything."

"So what story are you two wanting to hear?" Their mom looked back and forth between them.

Chapter 44

Jeremiah

"We really shouldn't be doing this." I don't even know why I bothered to say anything. Millie's mind was made up, so what I said made no difference. I backed out of the overgrown mesquite trees where we stashed our motorcycles and helmets and squinted at the sun's rays peeking over the hillside.

"You didn't have to come with me," Millie whispered. I don't know why. There was no one anywhere around.

"Well, I sure wasn't going to let you go alone."

"Why didn't you just tell me not to go?" She couldn't even get that sentence out without laughing.

"No kidding?" I said. "Look, let's just get this over with. You and I both know telling you not to go would have done no good."

"Come on, Jeremiah." She pulled the breakfast sandwiches out of her backpack. "You could at least enjoy the adventure. Let's eat first."

Millie peeled open the sandwich Mom wrapped for her and was just about ready to take a bite. "Wait!" I yelled. The look on her face made the whole risky trip worth it.

"You scared me to death!"

Well, get used to it," I choked out the words around my laughter. "Since you're leading us into the path of disaster, get used to being scared to death. Anyway, we might as well pray first, for our breakfast and for safety."

"Oh, you're right." She closed the wrapper on her sandwich and her eyes.

"Oh God, save me from this sister you gave me," I said, thankful we could joke around even with God. I was tempted to sneak a look at Millie's face, but kept my eyes shut tight. "And thank you for the food You provided and please watch over us on our adventure this morning and give us wisdom to make right choices. Especially my sister. Amen. Ouch!" I barely finished the prayer before Millie slugged me in the arm.

"Give me my sandwich," I rubbed my arm and pulled bottles of orange juice from my fanny pack. "Mom said be back by 8:30, for chores and school."

"Don't remind me." Millie's words were muffled as she chewed a way too large bite of her egg and cheese sandwich. "Don't spoil my morning."

"Well, we've got a little over two hours. I figure it will take us 20 minutes to walk to the store from here, especially in these heavy boots."

"Twenty there, twenty back, and twenty minutes to ride home. That gives us an hour to investigate," Millie said.

"Less than an hour since we're using time enjoying a leisurely breakfast." I downed the rest of my orange juice. "At your suggestion I might add."

She didn't even take the bait and argue back. Instead, she jumped up and wiggled her backpack into place. "Come on," she motioned. "Let's hit the road."

I took one last look at our bikes, as we stepped away from the trees, to make sure they couldn't be seen from the road. Confident they were hidden I turned toward my sister and pointed boldly toward our destination.

"Onward!"

Despite the soft sand we trudged through, we made better time than expected as we approached the back side of the abandoned store property.

"Let's watch where we're stepping," Millie said, "so we don't cover up tracks that might tell us something."

"Look, I already see tracks."

Millie stared in the direction I pointed, then looked back at me, eyes wide. "Those are semi-truck tracks."

"Exactly," I said. "And I'm wondering if it's the truck we've been hearing at night, the one without lights."

"Look!" Millie whispered. "There's two people. I wonder if it's the same ones you saw the other day."

I edged a little closer, hugging the brush-covered fence line of the property, so the shrubs would hide us. Millie followed at a distance.

Once I got close enough to see the couple peering into the windows of the store, I knew I had seen the woman before. But it sure wasn't here. My heart beat hard as I turned back to my sister.

"It's Julia," I whispered. "The nurse."

Chapter 45

Millie

"No way!" Millie looked up from her science textbook and stared across the dining room table at her brother.

He didn't budge. His nose was glued in the sci-fi novel he was devouring. That boy could lose himself, forgetting the rest of the world with whatever novel he was immersed in. Millie nudged his foot under the table, once, twice, then a third time, hard enough he couldn't ignore.

"What?" He looked up as if suddenly realizing someone else was in the room with him.

"There is no way that was Julia."

"That's a delayed reaction, don't you think?" He shoved a bookmark in between the pages and set the book aside, picking up his pencil and jotting some words in his notebook.

"What are you writing?" Millie said.

Jeremiah grinned. "I'm writing in my journal that my sister doesn't believe I know what I'm talking about."

"No, really," she said. "Are you writing something about what's going on?"

"Yes," he said, scribbling a few more sentences. "I'm writing about what's going on in my book so when I work on my book report I'll remember what to say." He reached over and grabbed for Millie's notebook, but she shoved it out of his reach. "You should try it sometime, you know. Take notes on your schoolwork instead of your detective work. It comes in handy if you actually want to learn something."

Jeremiah let his pencil flop to the table where it rolled to the edge. He opened his book again, but Millie slammed it shut.

"Tell me, it isn't so, Jeremiah. Why would Julia get mixed up in whatever is going on at that old store? I mean, she's a nurse. She's supposed to be respectable. Besides, she acted like she knew nothing about the store being closed down the other day."

"Hey," Jeremiah whispered. "I'm as surprised as you are. That's why I wanted to get out of there so fast. I didn't want to take a chance on her seeing us."

"Did you get a good look at the man? Was it the phony cop?"

"No, I didn't recognize him."

"Maybe it was her husband. He might be in on this too."

"Well, she sure had me fooled," Jeremiah said. "At the hospital and at Paisley's house the other day, she seemed like someone you could trust. Not like someone that would sneak around a closed down store."

"And what about those kids you saw the other day, do you think she has something to do with them being there?"

"I'm clueless." Jeremiah opened his book.

"Well, that I've always known." Millie threw her pencil at his book. "Come on, do you have to be such a bookworm? We've got problems to figure out."

"My biggest problem," Jeremiah pointed at her. "Is trying to figure out how to get my schoolwork done with your constant distractions."

"Millie, how is your schoolwork coming?" She could tell she was giving her mom that deer-in-the-headlights look when she turned to her. She was so surprised at the sudden appearance of her mom, it left her without a response.

“Uh-huh, I thought so,” their mom said as she reached into a cabinet, pulling out a big crock pot.

Millie sighed and turned a page in her science book. There went any chance to talk more to her brother if Mom was getting ready to put dinner in the slow cooker. She surprised herself by discovering something interesting in the passage she was reading and was just getting engrossed in science when her mom’s words startled her.

“What did you kids think of the nurse, Julia?” Millie’s stomach flip-flopped and she wondered if her mom had heard them talking. Mom smiled at both of them. “I like her a lot,” she said.

Chapter 46

Jeremiah

"Mom is a good judge of character." I'm not sure if I was trying to convince Millie or myself. I pulled the plates out of the kitchen cabinet and handed them to Millie. She took them without responding, so I continued. "She's always had some sort of special sense for figuring people out."

"Discernment," Millie said as she set the plates around the table.

"What?" I followed behind her with silverware and napkins.

"That's what it's called. Mom says she has the gift of discernment." Millie brought glasses over to the table and plopped them all down in one spot. "I think her discernment is off on this one, though." She picked up a glass and held it in mid-air, staring out the window.

"Well, maybe if she knew that Julia was snooping around the store today, she'd have a different opinion."

"That's not how discernment works," Millie said. "It doesn't have to be based on facts, it's a feeling."

"Okay," I picked up the glasses and set them on all the placemats while Millie still stood frozen. "Then her feelings are off on this one."

"What if we're wrong?" Millie set the glass down and stared at me. "What if that wasn't Julia at the store, maybe just someone who looked like her? We weren't that close."

"Trust me. It was her."

Millie stared, unbelieving.

"Look, believe what you want. I know what I saw."

"It's not that I don't . . ."

"Boy, does it smell good in here! Caleb, let's go tell Mom we're starving!" Dad and Caleb passed through the kitchen like two hungry animals on the prowl.

"It's not that I . . ." Millie tried to finish, but soon Dad and Caleb were back with Mom in tow.

We joined everyone at the table, forced to stop our conversation for now.

"So, did Mom tell you two about the adventure she discovered for you?" Dad didn't look our way after the prayer, as he focused on piling his plate high with beef.

I looked over at Millie, who didn't seem to know any more than I did. Mom buttered a dinner roll for Caleb. "No, I didn't get a chance to tell them yet, Max."

"Well, I could have figured that out for myself by their lack of response." He chuckled as he scooped carrots onto the side of his plate. "They probably wouldn't even be here at the table with us if they knew what treasure awaited them."

"What are you talking about?"

"The meteorite, Jeremiah." He motioned toward the dining room window. "It's out there somewhere in the desert waiting for you two."

Chapter 47

Millie

"Wait a minute." Millie looked from her dad to her mom. "You mean what Mom was telling us out by the fire the other night is true?"

"Well, young lady." Mom pretended to be hurt. "Are you saying you didn't believe me?"

"Oh, Mom. I didn't mean it like that."

"Explain it for us then, Millie," Jeremiah said. "What does it mean when you sound so surprised that something Mom said was true?"

The family enjoyed a laugh at Millie's expense as she looked around the table, speechless.

"I have to admit," Jeremiah said. "I found Mom's explanation of the ghost lights being a meteor a little too simple. Who knew it was just an atmospheric phenomenon?"

"Oh, my gosh!" Millie blurted out. "What have we here? A walking, talking dictionary?"

"I told you, sister dear." Jeremiah took a bite of his dinner roll. "You should try paying attention to your schoolwork once in a while."

Millie threw a dinner roll across the table at her brother. "Get real, you expect me to believe that was in your school assignment today?"

"Millicent!" Mom said. "When are you going to learn some manners?"

"I'm sorry, Mom."

"Yeah, Millie," Caleb said. "You will set a bad example for me."

Millie laughed and reached over to hug Caleb.

"And no," Jeremiah said. "It wasn't in my assignment today." He smiled as he scooped a second helping of the casserole. "It was on my vocabulary list last week."

"So, if you two are finished arguing over schoolwork and the trustworthiness of your mother, maybe you'd like to know what she discovered today," Dad said.

"Okay, well, hold on," Jeremiah said. "Because I admit I was only half listening the other night when you said something about a meteor. Are you saying that there aren't really ghost lights? It was a meteor shooting through the sky that people saw?"

"That's what I'm saying." Mom picked up a piece of paper next to her plate. Millie watched her unfold the paper she hadn't even noticed laying on the table.

"I found this online today and printed it out to share with you." Mom held the paper up and read, "Scientists Search For Fallen Meteorite."

Millie reached over to grab the paper, but her Mom pulled it away. "Millie, it's polite to ask, not just grab it out of my hand."

"Yeah, Millie," Caleb said. "Don't set bad examples."

Okay, the first time Millie thought it was funny, but this time she was not laughing with the rest of the family.

"I'm sorry, Mom." It took so much effort to admit fault, but she was dying to know what the rest of that paper said.

"I'll summarize it for both of you."

"And, you, young man," Dad looked at Caleb, "please leave the disciplining to the parents."

Caleb smiled up at their Dad. "Does that mean you're my parents, too?"

Dad reached over and tousled his hair. "Well, Caleb, I'd be honored for you to call us your parents while your mom is away."

Caleb grabbed hold of their dad's hand and looked toward their mom. "Well, Mom, tell us what the scientists said fell."

Millie loved the warm feeling that spread through the room. She watched Caleb glowing as he listened to the good-natured laughter around the table. But enough of the warm fuzzy feelings. It was time to move forward with the information gathering. "So what does the rest of the article say, Mom?"

"At 8:02 p.m. Saturday evening, a bright meteoritic bolide was . . ."

"A meteoritic bolide, what in the world are they talking about?" Millie interrupted.

"Let her finish, Millie," Jeremiah said.

But before Mom could resume reading, the sound of car tires crunching on the gravel outside interrupted them.

Chapter 48

Jeremiah

"It's Deputy Black!" Caleb shouted from where he stood by the window.

I jumped out of my chair, nearly knocking it over, and ran to the door. Maybe he had been to see Caleb's mom and had news for us.

Caleb beat me to the door and was outside hugging Griffin before the rest of us made it out to the porch.

"Do you have news for us?" Millie said. I could tell by the look on his face he did, but he just nodded his head as Caleb clung to him.

Griffin knelt down to talk to the boy face to face. "And how are you doing? You look like you've grown since you've been here."

Caleb stood straight and puffed out his chest. "I have! I'm having so much fun here. Thank you for bringing me here!"

Griffin stood back up. "You're sure welcome, Caleb," he said as he reached out to shake hands with Dad. "Well, what's everybody up to today?"

Millie groaned, and I gave her a dirty look. I knew she just wanted to get right down to the business of finding out whether or not Caleb had a sister, but she must know Griffin couldn't talk in front of Caleb.

"Well, Norah was just telling the kids the news about the scientists searching for a meteorite in this area."

"No kidding?" Griffin said. "Nearby?"

"Somewhere in or around Dry Brook, according to the news report I found online today," Mom said.

"That must be what sparked all the recent talk about ghost lights," Griffin said. "How about that? It wasn't ghostly at all. Just a few people who had the fantastic opportunity to view a meteor falling from the sky."

"Kinda disappointing if you ask me," Millie said.

"Not exciting enough for my sister. Ghost lights sounded so much more adventurous when there wasn't a scientific explanation."

"It would be a big adventure if you were the one to find the meteorite," Mom said. "Don't you think, Millie?"

"It's not likely that would happen." She moaned.

"Well, why not? The news report said they believe it's in a two-mile area between the Superstition Hills, Dry Brook Badlands and Dos Palmas Wash."

"That's close to here," Griffin said.

"Your mom says they're encouraging people to search for it, Millie." Dad patted her on the shoulder.

For as annoying as she could be, none of us liked seeing her discouraged.

"I'll bet we could find it, Millie. In fact, it sounds so educational, Mom might even give us extra riding time tomorrow." I looked over at Mom. "Wouldn't that count toward schoolwork?"

"Well, let me give that some thought. Maybe you can start in the morning by reading the complete news report, then mapping out a plan for where to search."

Millie groaned. "Oh Mom, do you have to wring all the fun out of it?"

Dad and Griffin laughed, but I kept my chuckle to myself so I didn't get a dirty look.

I saw Griffin looking at his watch, and Mom must have seen it too.

"Caleb," she bent over to look him in the eye. "How would you like to come in with me and test the dessert before we serve it to everyone?" Mention sweets and Caleb would do whatever you asked.

Griffin winked at Mom as she took Caleb's hand and headed inside.

Millie practically rushed Griffin, and Dad and I weren't far behind in gathering around him.

"So I take it you have news for us?" Dad said.

"I sure do," Griffin looked around, making eye contact with each one of us. "I had an interesting visit with Caleb's mom today."

Chapter 49

Finally. Millie couldn't believe after all this waiting they were going to get some answers about the mystery sister Caleb kept talking about. At least she thought they were.

"Before I get into that, what is happening with Paisley?" Griffin said. "I've had no contact since Julia and I left the other evening."

Millie cringed at the mention of Julia. She looked over at Jeremiah and knew by the look on his face he felt the same way.

"What?" Griffin said. "Is there bad news about Paisley?" Millie tensed. She should have known with Griffin being a cop he was probably aware of even slight changes in demeanor.

"No," their Dad said, oblivious to the silent communication between them. "In fact, they've gone to the city to see the specialist Julia recommended. Their appointment is tomorrow, but they're staying in town for a few days."

Relieved her dad hadn't caught on to their attitude, Millie avoided looking at him. She didn't want to answer questions about their reaction to the mention of Julia. That would open up a whole can of worms about what was going on at the abandoned store. Not to mention the trouble it might get them into.

"We better get to the news about Caleb's mom before he comes back out," Millie said.

"Good idea." Griffin motioned for them to follow him away from the house. "To make a long story short, she says there is no sister."

"Why would that be a long story?" Millie asked.

"You tell me. My thoughts are there is more to the story than she is telling. She talked all around this sister thing. She rambled about Caleb having quite an imagination, how he always wanted a sister, how he would pretend he had a sister. But she was adamant there is no sister."

"Did you tell her what he said about the light being a signal?" Jeremiah asked.

"I sure did. She laughed. Said she couldn't understand why he would make up a story like that. Insisted Caleb is her only child."

"Boy, she did turn that into a long story," their Dad said.

"You got that right. In fact the only reason the story finally ended is because I told her I had to leave."

"Wow," Millie said. "What do you think? Do you believe her?"

"Good question. And the answer is, I'm not sure."

"But why would she lie about it, if he had a sister?" Jeremiah asked.

"To protect herself," their Dad said. "If what Caleb is saying is true, then something is very odd about the situation."

"But wouldn't you have heard about a sister long before this?" Millie said. "You've known the family for a while, haven't you?"

"About a year, and yes, it seems like I would have heard about another child. But there was never any mention of it until you folks told me about it."

"Hey, what about the deputy that was with you the other day?" Millie said. "The day Paisley got sick."

"Leon?"

"I don't know his name. Would he know anything about Caleb's family?"

"He wasn't a deputy, Millie," Jeremiah said. "He's Border Patrol."

"Border Patrol?" Millie looked from Jeremiah back to Griffin. "What was he doing here? How come you were out riding together?"

"I brought him here to meet your dad," Griffin said. "I had the day off and rode along with him while he was on patrol. And you sure ask a lot of questions."

"No kidding!" Jeremiah said. Millie ignored both of their comments.

"Why was he patrolling this area? I've never seen Border Patrol around here."

"They're around," Griffin said. "You better crank up your spy senses, you're slipping there, young lady."

Millie ignored the laughter from all of them and pushed for information. "What are they looking for?"

"What do you think, Millie?" Jeremiah said. "Smuggling. Drugs. People. Why do you think we go through the border checkpoint every time we come home from the grocery store?"

Chapter 50

Jeremiah

I could tell Millie didn't like me implying she should have known all that. As annoying as she could be, I felt bad when my teasing upset her. I turned to Griffin. "Millie has a good idea, though. Do you think Leon might know anything about Caleb's family?"

"He just might," Griffin said. "He's worked this area for quite a few years. Even before Caleb was born."

"Deputy Black!" Caleb threw open the front door and leaped off the porch, running toward Griffin. "Mom said to invite you in for dessert."

"Mom?" Griffin looked in Dad's direction.

"Yeah!" Caleb tugged on Griffin's hand. "Max and Norah said I could call them my parents while I'm here."

"That is a great idea." Griffin smiled at Caleb and took hold of his hand. "So lead me to the dessert that Mom has waiting for us."

We sat around the table enjoying cinnamon crumb cake and vanilla ice cream. Caleb had cinnamon all over his chin and cheeks. He was looking happier every day. Quite a change from the quiet, sad little boy who moved in a few months ago.

"Hey, Mom," Millie said. "Can you finish reading the news report now? Griffin might like to hear it."

"I sure would, I've always been interested in astronomy, but never been lucky enough to see a meteor." Griffin sliced himself a second piece of crumb cake and looked at Mom. "This sure is delicious. I might have to get me a wife one of these days."

Mom laughed as she picked up the paper and continued reading. "Anyone who saw the meteoritic fireball Saturday evening, and especially anyone who was in the area of Dry Brook or Dos Palmas Wash at the time of sighting, should contact either Professor James R. Goles or Professor Gordon G. Arnold at the Space Museum and Science Center. Also, anyone who intends to visit the area, should keep their eyes open for an object coated with a shiny black fusion crust which looks as if it might have fallen from the sky. The meteorite is of great scientific value."

"Wow," I said. "I can't believe we live right in the area where such an important scientific event happened."

"I guess it's too late to go searching tonight?" Millie turned her puppy dog eyes on Dad.

"You guessed right, Millie." Dad reached over and patted her hand on the table.

"It's safer not to go out after dark anyway," Griffin looked from Dad to Mom. "Best to keep the kids near the house after sundown for the time being."

Chapter 51

Millie

"Why do you think Griffin said what he did about not going out after dark?"

Jeremiah took a long swig of his water, then twisted the lid back on and leaned against his motorcycle. "I'm guessing it has something to do with illegal border crossing, either drugs or people."

"Did you talk with the Border Patrol guy the other day?"

"I got to meet him when Griffin brought him in the shop. He seemed to be looking for something specific in this area, but he didn't give details. He said one thing that kind of worried me."

"What was that?" Millie scrounged in her backpack, then brought out a couple packs of trail mix.

Jeremiah took the trail mix she offered and struggled to rip it open. "Leon told me if I see anything suspicious I should let him know."

Millie took the little package back and ripped the top off.

"How do you do that?" Jeremiah dumped trail mix into his palm, then tossed it into his mouth.

"Talent," Millie talked around the nuts and raisins she chomped on. "What did you say when he asked if you'd seen anything suspicious?"

"Well, I felt guilty, that's for sure. But thankfully he didn't ask if I'd seen anything, he just said if I ever do, I should let him know."

"Were you thinking about the old store?" Millie crumpled her trail mix packet, stood and wiped the dirt and twigs from her riding pants.

Jeremiah did the same, then straddled his motorcycle and grabbed his helmet from where it was hanging on the handlebar. "That's exactly what I was thinking." He balanced the helmet on the gas tank and leaned his elbow on it. "If he had asked me directly if I'd seen anything suspicious, I would have had to tell him."

"Yeah, I see what you mean. I guess this way you weren't actually lying."

"No, but I sure wasn't being honest either." He picked the helmet up and tugged it down over his head.

"Do you think we should tell Griffin what we saw?" Millie copied his actions, then fastened the strap under her chin. "I want to search around the store more. And if we tell, we won't be able to do that."

"And what if we don't tell, and we get in big trouble, or worse, get hurt or something while we're searching?" Jeremiah pulled out the kick starter. "Isn't it good enough to search for a meteorite?" He kicked the starter, and his bike roared to life.

"That's why I wanted Paisley to search with me," Millie thought. "She wouldn't bail out on me. At least she wouldn't have if she hadn't gotten sick."

Out loud she said, "I'll think about it while we ride." Millie kicked her bike over and yelled over the sound of the engine. "We sure haven't had any luck yet this morning."

Jeremiah wasn't looking at her, his eyes focused on something behind her.

"Millie, look over there."

Chapter 52

Jeremiah

I cut the engine and just about fell when I jumped off my bike and ran toward the object glistening in the sun. Millie followed right behind.

We were both huffing and puffing by the time we got midway up the hill.

"Check this out, Millie." I knelt down, shielding my eyes from the glare. Millie moved around until she stood in just the right spot to block the sun from shining on the metal.

"Millie, it's a bumper from an old car."

"It looks like it's polished."

"How could that be?" I picked it up. "This thing is heavy. How could it be so shiny laying out here in the wilderness? It doesn't even look weathered."

"Look," Millie pointed to both ends of the bumper. "They're weathered."

"So someone keeps the middle section polished." I set the bumper back in the brush. It looked like someone moved it often, not like something that was laying in one place for a long time. There were several areas where the brush look flattened and the dirt gouged as the metal dug into it.

"Jeremiah, this is the area Caleb keeps pointing to. We're right on the hillside. Look, if we turn and look to the north, our property should be over there somewhere. We'd be able to see the reflection from a few miles away."

"Millie," I whispered, wondering if someone might be nearby. "Someone keeps the bumper polished and moves it around. Maybe there is a sister."

Her eyes were large as she stared around the area, then back at me. "And she could be the one polishing the bumper. And maybe she picks it up to reflect the sun."

"Yeah, because right now, the early morning sun reflected from where it was. But Caleb has been seeing it at different times of the day. So someone is picking it up and causing it to reflect."

"I hope our bikes are safe back there," Millie looked down the hill where we left them. "I feel like someone might be watching us."

"I wondered the same thing, like is someone nearby?"

"Let's look for footprints." Millie picked our helmets up from the ground. I took mine as we walked.

The ground was hard, and we couldn't even see our own prints. I looked toward home.

"Millie, if Dad would let us use those expensive high-powered binoculars he had for his job, I bet we could see all the way to this hill from our house."

"If we could look when the light was reflecting we might see someone holding this bumper up." Millie clapped her hands, while jumping up and down. "That would be awesome. If there is a sister, we might spot her."

"Yeah, but that's a big 'if' for Dad to let us use those. I think I will ask Caleb why he thinks his sister is up here and see what he says."

"If we have a really good reason I'm sure Dad would let us use them. And this is a really good reason."

“Well, Millie, you’re the one to ask him. Or should I say beg him?” As we headed toward our motorcycles, a drone caught my eye. It was circling the area south of us. “Millie, look at that drone.”

“Jeremiah!” She pointed. “Something just fell from it.”

I watched a box falling to the ground as the drone circled, then increased elevation and headed south.

Chapter 53

Millie

"Jeremiah, let's ride over and find that box," Millie called over her shoulder as she jogged toward the motorcycles.

Her brother caught up with her. "I don't know, Millie. We're supposed to be looking for the meteorite."

"Yeah, well, we haven't found it yet and at least if we find the box we will have found something."

"It's not safe. They were probably dropping the box for someone expecting it."

"Look around," Millie said. "Do you see anyone? Besides, I think it just fell from the drone. You know, by accident."

"How would you even know?"

Millie had her helmet on and motorcycle running. "Humor me." She yelled over the sound of the engine. "Let's ride in that direction a little way." She took off before her brother could argue.

Millie struggled to keep her bike upright as she maneuvered around the growing number of sagebrush and creosote bushes the higher they rode up the mountain. She wasn't used to leading when she and Jeremiah went riding and venturing into the desert mountains with so much tangled shrubbery and no trails to speak of tested her skill, or lack of it. She looked back for Jeremiah, but lost control. The handlebars twisted hard to the right, tossing her off the bike and into a thorny bush.

"Jeremiah!" What a relief to see him so close.

Her brother grabbed hold of her arms and tugged. "Cat's Claw!" she yelled as she picked at the thorns clinging to her riding jersey.

"What are you talking about?" Jeremiah said once she was out of the bush and standing.

"That stupid bush." Millie brushed at the leaves and twigs on her shirt and pants. "That's what it's called."

"Since when do you know something?" Jeremiah laughed as he picked her motorcycle up.

"Botany Adventure." Millie took her helmet off and set it on the seat of her bike. She shrugged out of her backpack. "I need some water."

"I must have missed out on that adventure." Jeremiah grabbed a water bottle out of her backpack.

"Mom was trying to make science more fun for me last year." She guzzled down the water. "And it worked. That's how I know the name of this stupid plant that grabbed hold of me."

"Are you okay?"

"Yeah, I'm fine. And you will not believe this," Millie wiped her mouth on her sleeve and tucked the empty water bottle into her backpack. "I'm ready to go home."

Millie zipped the backpack and slung it into place on her back, then turned to see why Jeremiah hadn't responded to her startling decision about going home.

"Jeremiah? Where are you?"

Chapter 54

Jeremiah

Millie would not believe this. I took off running while she was jabbering about something. I wanted to get back with the box in time to surprise her when she finished fiddling with her backpack and turned around.

Running in riding boots was hard, especially dodging bushes and boulders. I sure didn't want any Cat's Claw plants grabbing hold of me. I couldn't believe my sister actually learned something in science.

The box was bigger than I expected, but when I picked it up it hardly weighed anything. There were no labels or marks of any kind. Just a plain brown box that fell from the sky.

"Millie!" I yelled out as I turned to head back. This took a little longer than I thought, and she might be worried. "Millie!" I rounded the bush she had crashed into and could see her looking all around.

I knew the second she spotted me.

"Jeremiah!" she screamed and ran toward me. "You found it! You found it!"

Well, if anyone else was in the area, they would know, too, that I found the box.

Millie took it from me as soon as I got to her. "It's so light," she said.

"Yeah, I wonder what we should do with it? It doesn't even have a name on it."

"Let's take it home." Millie pulled on her helmet.

"It's not ours," Jeremiah said.

"It is now." Millie straddled her motorcycle and balanced the box on her gas tank.

"I don't think so," I grabbed the box and set it on my bike, then pulled my helmet on. "If we're taking it home, I'll ride with it. At least it will get there in one piece."

"Oh, you're real funny," Millie said and then kicked her bike over. She revved the engine and sprayed dirt and pebbles on me as she steered the bike around to head downhill.

That girl. She could be impossible sometimes. Why couldn't I have gotten a nice, calm, quiet girl like Paisley for a sister? I felt a lump in my throat at the thought of Paisley. She was probably going through the testing right now. "Oh God," I prayed out loud in my helmet as I followed Millie down the hillside. "Please take care of Paisley. Please tell the doctors what to do."

"Mom! Dad!" Millie raced through the house yelling for our parents as I followed carrying the box. "We found something!"

Dad and Mom came hurrying out of the office, meeting up with us in the kitchen. "Did you find the meteorite?" Mom asked. She looked so excited, I hated to tell her no. So I let Millie do that.

"We found something better," Millie said. "And it fell from the sky too!"

CHAPTER 55

"What in the world?" Mom said when Jeremiah set the box on the table.

"You say this fell from the sky, Millie?" Dad looked unbelieving. "Jeremiah, is that right?"

"Oh, so you believe Jeremiah, but not me?"

"Well, face it, sis, you get some wild ideas, sometimes." Jeremiah gave her one of those patronizing looks she hated. But right now she was so eager to see what was in the box, she ignored the pest.

"Well, we were riding south looking for…" Jeremiah started.

"The meteorite!" Millie interrupted. She didn't want them to know they were looking for the shiny object that Caleb talked about. She wanted to make sure Mom trusted them to keep going out in search of the meteorite. There were so many interesting things waiting for them to discover out there in the desert.

Jeremiah took a deep breath. "I love being interrupted. Said no one ever." He gave her a dirty look.

"Well, that's quite a story," Dad said after they related the strange events of the morning. Not including finding the bumper.

"So can we open the box now?" Millie looked from one parent to the other.

"No."

"No?" Millie said a bit too loudly. "Why not?"

"It isn't ours," Dad said. "And it could very well be connected to a crime."

"I have the business card from Griffin's friend Leon," Mom said. "I saw it with your keys and wallet, so I filed it."

"Thanks, Norah. I think we should call him."

"Why not just call Griffin?" Millie asked.

"This seems like something the Border Patrol should check out," Dad said. "I've read about smugglers dropping items from planes and drones for their associates on the ground."

"Oh, Max!" Mom's hands went up to her face, her eyes opening wide in fright. "They could have been in danger." She looked at both kids. "Did either of you see anyone in the area?"

"No one," Millie said.

"We looked all around us too, and there was no sign of anyone," Jeremiah said. "I thought maybe it dropped from the drone by mistake."

It didn't take long for Leon to show up.

"Thanks for the call," he said after he greeted them. "I was on my way to check out a potential drop. They caught the drone on radar when it crossed the border. Sounds like your kids made my job a little easier."

He looked at the box sitting on the table, then over at Jeremiah. "Boy, you really paid attention when I said to call if you saw anything suspicious."

Jeremiah smiled, but Millie wasn't going to let him get all the praise. "Well, it didn't take a rocket scientist to know that a box falling from the sky was suspicious."

They all laughed, while Leon pulled out a knife and sliced through the tape on the box top. He looked inside and whistled, then spoke, almost to himself.

"Well, I've heard about this, but I've never seen it for myself."

Chapter 56

Jeremiah

I watched as Leon pulled a slender potato chip can out of the box. He laid it on its side on the table and we watched, stunned, as the can moved back and forth.

Millie gasped. “What is inside that thing?”

Leon pulled a pair of gloves from a pouch on his belt and slipped his hands into them before lifting the potato chip can from the table. He pulled the plastic lid off and tipped the can with one hand. A large lizard wrapped in masking tape slipped out of the can into his other hand. He dropped the can, then used both hands to hold the reptile.

“Oh my goodness,” Mom said. “That poor creature.”

“What is going on?” Millie asked.

“Smugglers.” Leon peeled the masking tape off the bound legs. “Lizards are just one of many animals sold on the black market.” He looked up at their parents, shaking his head. “It’s a billion dollar business around the globe, smuggling wildlife.”

They watched as the lizard stretched and moved his legs. "Do you have some cardboard boxes I can put them in?"

"Them?" I looked inside the box. My mouth dropped open when I saw 15 or 20 more potato chip cans. "Millie, look at this."

She had tears rolling down her cheeks, which explained why she had been so quiet. I never knew she had a soft spot for critters. She reached out and touched the head of the one Leon held. "I used to own a big lizard, kind of like this one."

Mom put her arm around Millie's shoulders. "Oh, honey, I'm so sorry. This must be extra hard for you."

Dad returned with Caleb in tow. They both carried boxes. "Come on, Caleb, let's get more." He steered him away before Caleb could see what the boxes were for.

"How about if Millie and I get some branches and shrubbery to put in the box?"

"You go get that stuff," Millie said. "I'm going to cut up some banana and see what veggies we have that lizards can eat. I remember what they like from when I owned one."

"Whatever happened to your lizard?"

I knew by the look on her face, I shouldn't have asked.

"We'll talk about it another time, Jeremiah." She was already peeling the banana.

"I'm going out to my car to radio this in," Leon said. "Then I'll get the rest of them out of the cans." He looked over at me. "If you don't mind, get enough for all these boxes."

Caleb helped me carry in the branches, rocks and bits of shrubbery. I found enough to house an army of lizards.

Leon followed us inside. He watched as Millie, Caleb, and I made nice little habitats in each of the boxes. The kitchen had turned into a reptile preserve.

"This is nice, kids," Leon said. He looked at each one of us. Mom and Dad looked proud.

Then Leon looked over at my parents. "Now, I've got a huge favor to ask."

Chapter 57

Millie

Millie hoped against hope Leon would ask her parents the same thing she wanted to ask. In a rare show of self-discipline, she kept her mouth shut, waiting to hear what he had to say. It was well worth it.

"It really impressed my supervisor how Jeremiah and Millie," he reached out and patted Caleb's head, "and Caleb too, have all pitched in to help."

"I would have to agree," Dad smiled at all three of the kids.

Leon cleared his voice and nodded. "In fact, he's so impressed he wanted me to ask if you all would be willing to keep the lizards here until our Customs Field Officer can get out to assess the situation and make arrangements to transport and care for the lizards."

"Yes!" Millie shouted.

"I'm surprised you kept quiet this long, Mil," Jeremiah said.

"Please, Mom! Please, Dad!" Millie turned pleading eyes to her parents. "This would mean so much to me."

"Do you have any idea how long that will be, Leon?" Dad asked.

He hesitated, rubbed his chin, then took a deep breath. "Honestly? It could be a few weeks to a month or more. He covers a big territory that encompasses all the rural communities out this way."

"Even better!" Millie knelt down next to the box that contained the freed lizard. "Can we let the others loose now?"

Leon touched her shoulder. "Not just yet," he said. He looked at her mom and dad.

"Sorry to push, but your answer has a bearing on whether I free the others now."

"You mean you'll leave them in the canisters if we can't keep them here?" Millie moaned. "That's so not fair."

"It's a practical matter, Millie. I appreciate all of you gathering up the boxes, but I wouldn't be able to fit them in my car."

Millie could see Dad and Mom whispering to each other while Leon talked with her. Surely they wouldn't force these poor reptiles to stay bound in the containers.

"Dad," Jeremiah spoke up. "I know Millie and I could take care of them and she's had a lizard before, so she knows what to do."

Millie wanted to hug her brother, but she stayed put on the floor next to Chippie. She smiled. There was no way she could let this little critter go now that she had already named him. She peered in the box and watched the lizard looking up at her.

"He trusts me," Millie said. "I can tell."

Leon watched Millie interact with the reptile. "You know, I believe he does."

Millie held back tears. This reminded her so much of the pet she said goodbye to several years ago in foster care. She remembered crying for weeks when she didn't get to take the lizard with her when she moved to a new foster home.

Dad and Mom were still whispering, but Millie couldn't wait any longer. "Please, Mom and Dad! Please don't make me say goodbye to Chippie!"

Jeremiah burst out laughing. "Chippie? That's hilarious."

Mom knelt down next to her and smiled. "I know where you got that name."

Caleb picked up the potato chip can. "I know too, Millie. 'Cause he came out of a chip can." He sat down next to Millie, staring into the box. "I love Chippie, too." He reached into the box, then jerked his hand back the lizard hissed. Caleb glared into the box. "Bad Chippie!"

"Oh dear," Mom said.

Millie cringed. It seemed like her mom had been close to agreeing, and now she'd probably say no because it was too dangerous.

"Caleb, you were smart to pull your hand back from the box." Dad joined them on the floor. "We must be careful with these creatures. They're scared and probably angry too. And they have good reason to be angry. Someone has mistreated them."

Millie felt hope rising in her. Dad talked like they would keep them. She was afraid to look up in his face, afraid to ask. She wanted to hold on to the hope that Dad would say yes they could take care of them. As long as she didn't know yet, she could still hope.

Chapter 58

Jeremiah

I was torn between not wanting to spend my days taking care of needy reptiles that were just waiting to bite my finger off in retaliation for being captured and stuffed into canisters, but not wanting to see my sister fall apart if we couldn't keep them.

Millie looked ready to cry, and it was crazy how that lizard seemed to bond with her already. It was clear though he hadn't bonded and probably wouldn't bond with Caleb. Wow, that hiss sounded crazy mean.

Dad patted Millie on the shoulder, then turned to face Leon.

"We'll be happy to help." I expected Millie to go bonkers with excitement, but instead she cried. Whew, she wore me out trying to keep up with her emotions. I felt sorry for the guy she might marry someday. I hoped all girls weren't like this.

Mom stayed next to Millie with one arm draped around her shoulders. Leon pulled his gloves back on and took another canister out of the box. Caleb lost interest after getting hissed at and disappeared into another room. I sure wasn't going to ask if I could help pull those angry critters out of the canisters, so I was content to watch as one by one they were freed and placed in their new homes.

Millie went from box to box, checking on the welfare of each one, placing food and water. I don't know where she came up with all those water bowls. It was as if she had been expecting a tsunami of reptiles to descend on us and she had the supplies to care for them.

Before long, all the canisters were empty. There were 16 live lizards and two we would bury. I'm sure if Millie gets her way, it will be with a full-on funeral with music and a speech before burial.

"Jeremiah, will you go tell Caleb lunch is ready?" I hadn't noticed Mom making sandwiches and setting the table while we were busy with lizard rescue.

"He's sound asleep on the floor in his room surrounded by his cars," I said when I returned to the kitchen. Everyone, including Leon, was seated when I joined them at the table.

Dad said grace, and Millie and I dug in before anyone else. My appetite raged after our adventurous morning. Millie hardly talked since we found out we were keeping the lizards. I think she was so overcome with joy she couldn't talk. Wow, I wish she could be this overcome all the time. I snickered at my joke.

"What's so funny over there, Jeremiah?" Dad said. "And pass me that bowl of chips while you share your joke."

Hmm, I needed to get out of this without hurting Millie's feelings. Sometimes I didn't care, but today wasn't one of those days. I passed the chip bowl down his way. "I was just thinking how funny Caleb looked sound asleep with cars in both his hands." Mom enjoyed that, and I sure hoped God would forgive a lie like that.

"I can't tell you all how much I appreciate you helping with the lizards," Leon said. "And to feed me a delicious lunch too, well, it's turned out to be a great day." He wiped his mouth and dropped his napkin on his plate. "I can tell you not all our days are great. In fact, some are very much not so great."

Mom nodded. "I can imagine you see some tough things in your line of work."

"Say, Leon," Dad said. "On a different topic, we wanted to ask you about Caleb's family. Griffin said you might be familiar with them."

"Sure, what do you want to know? I didn't get to know the boy as well as Griffin did, but I've known of the family for quite a few years."

Millie surprised me by coming alive. "Does Caleb have a sister?"

Chapter 59

Millie

"He does, but she didn't live with the family," Leon said.

"Where did she live?" Millie asked before anyone else could get a word out.

"Well, I take that back." Leon paused, as if remembering. "When the family first moved to this area, oh, say, five or six years ago, the sister lived with them. It was the girl and Caleb, who was quite a bit younger, and an on-again, off-again boyfriend of the mom's."

"So when did the sister move out?" Jeremiah glanced at Millie triumphantly. She smiled, knowing he was glad he beat her to a question for once.

"About a year or two ago. She went to live with her dad in some other state," Leon said. "I don't remember where."

"How do you know that's where she went?" Millie's question came out more like a challenge than a polite inquiry.

Leon looked startled, but it seemed to cause him to think. "Well, I guess I just took the mom's word for it. But now you got me thinking."

"Thinking?" Millie challenged again.

"Millicent." Mom was firm. "Stop interrogating, Leon."

Remembering the lizards he had just entrusted to her care, Millie felt ashamed. "I'm sorry."

He smiled. "It's okay, Millie. I'm impressed by your thoroughness. You might make an excellent detective someday."

"Okay," Jeremiah said, "now you both got me curious. What did Millie's question cause you to think about?"

Mom brought a plate of cookies to the table and set them in front of Leon and Dad. "She would have to do that," Millie thought. "Now he's distracted with oatmeal raisin cookies, and it will take forever to get an answer." He surprised Millie by reaching for a cookie and then just holding it while staring in space, like he'd gone back in time.

"I remember now that I had been by the house several times and not seen the girl. Don't remember her name." He stopped and looked at the cookie in his hand like he wasn't sure how it got there.

"Leon, would you like some coffee to go with that?"

He looked sheepish. "Actually, ma'am, I'd prefer a glass of milk." He looked over at Millie. "I never acquired a taste for coffee, but milk with cookies, now that's living."

Millie laughed politely, although she just wanted to get back to the story.

"So I asked the mom about the girl, said I hadn't seen her lately, when she used to be outside most of the time. She was always stacking rocks in piles or hunting for bugs. I remember I'd get such a kick out of seeing her puttering around outside when I would be in the area." He stopped talking and took a couple bites of the cookie when Mom set the glass of milk in front of him.

Millie decided she might as well join in and grabbed a few cookies. She would have preferred chocolate chips rather than raisins.

"So I never thought anything about the mom's answer until today." He looked over at Millie. "Something tells me you're suspicious about that answer, and now I am, too."

Millie was dying to ask another question, but she was close enough to Jeremiah for him to kick her under the table.

"When I asked the mom where the girl was . . . why can't I remember her name?" He stopped and stared into space. "Well, anyway, when I asked, I remember now the mom hesitated just a split second. Enough to make me think now that she was making up an answer. Then she blurted out something like 'oh she's gone with her dad, yeah, she's gone with her dad.'" He took a drink of milk and finished his cookie, then looked around the table at all of them. "She repeated herself after having to think about it. See what I mean about it seeming strange?"

"I sure do," Dad said.

"Well, I was suspicious," Millie said, "because she told Griffin she didn't have any other kids besides Caleb."

"What other kids besides me?" Caleb stood in the kitchen doorway, rubbing his eyes, his hair frazzled from sleep.

CHAPTER 60

Jeremiah

We were so engrossed in talk about Caleb's sister that we didn't notice him at the kitchen door. I felt bad that he heard us talking about his family and wondered how much he heard.

"Hey there, little buddy." I jumped up from my chair and went to greet him. "You slept right through lunch."

"I did?" he said, still rubbing his eyes.

Taking his other hand, I led him to the table. "You sure did, but I bet Mom will make a sandwich for you real quick."

Caleb spotted the cookies. His face lit up. "I can just eat cookies." He reached for the plate. "You don't have to go to all that trouble for me, Miss Norah." He looked over at Mom, then corrected himself with a huge smile. "I mean Mom!" Before she could answer, Caleb bit into a cookie. He looked over at Leon. "Miss Norah said I could call her Mom."

"Well, how about that?" Leon said.

"My mom's gone somewheres." He finished the cookie and grabbed another one before Mom could stop him. "Did you know that my mom was gone somewheres?" He directed his question to Leon.

Leon smiled. "I did and I'm sure glad you found such a great family to live with while she's gone."

"It's okay if she don't come back for a long, long time," Caleb talked around the bite of cookie he was chewing. He was as bad as Millie. Mom didn't even correct him, she was probably too concerned he might have heard us talking about his family. "I can just stay here the rest of my life if she can't come back." Caleb looked around the table and smiled, then back at Leon. "I'm happy here. Did you know that?"

We all laughed. "Well if I didn't know," Leon said, "I sure know it now."

Leon scooted his chair over and leaned close to him. "Caleb, I haven't seen your sister in a long time. Do you know where she moved to?"

Caleb reached for another cookie, but this time Mom was faster. She pulled the cookie plate away and placed a sandwich in front of him. "Peanut butter and strawberry jelly, Caleb. Your favorite."

Caleb took a big bite, then turned back to Leon, jelly on both sides of his mouth. "She knows I love strawberry jelly."

Leon wiped the edges of Caleb's mouth with a napkin.

"See why I like living here so much?" Caleb said, "They're nice to me." He took a few more bites, then looked back at Leon. "Sometimes my mom wasn't nice to me. You remember that, don't you?"

This was news to all of us. Leon looked upset. He took a deep breath before answering. "Well, your mom had some problems, Caleb. But she's taking care of those now and look what a special place she found for you to live."

"She didn't find this place," Caleb said. "Deputy Black said it was God who brought me here."

"Well, how about that?" Leon said. "God's pretty special now, isn't He?"

"Yeah, He is." Caleb finished the first half of his sandwich and eyed the cookie plate across the table. "I hope God will bring my sister here next." He bit into the other half of his sandwich and while chewing said, "I miss her."

"Do you know where she lives now?" Leon asked.

This was perfect with Leon here to get all this information. It helped because he knew Caleb's family. I felt funny asking questions of Caleb because it seemed like prying.

"Yeah," Caleb pointed. "She lives over on the mountain. Where the shiny thing is."

Chapter 61

Millie

"I can't believe we're getting to go with him to find Caleb's sister," Millie said as she fastened her seat belt in the back seat of the Border Patrol SUV.

"Millie, he's told you a hundred times, we're not going to search for her sister. We're just going to show him where we found the polished bumper."

Millie sighed. "A hundred times, Jeremiah? Isn't that a bit of an exaggeration?"

"Well, not by much," their Dad said and laughter filled the car. Only Millie wasn't laughing. She left that to Leon, her dad and her brother.

"Well, why can't we look for her while we're up there?"

"Quit whining," Jeremiah said.

"I'm not whining." Millie tried to defend herself, but even she recognized the whine this time. "Well, not too much, am I?"

"I know you're disappointed, Millie," Leon glanced at her in the mirror as he drove the car out the gate and down the dirt road. "I'd feel the same way if I were you, but it's too dangerous to search while I have all of you with me. The only reason you're here now is to show me where the bumper is and where you found the box. After that I'll bring the three of you back home and probably have Griffin accompany me when I go back to search the area."

"What will happen if you find her?" Millie said.

She saw Leon look over at her dad and then back to the paved road he had just turned onto. "What do you mean?" he said. Millie couldn't believe that adults could be just like kids. She figured it was clear what she meant, and he probably didn't want to answer the question. So just like a kid, he pretends he doesn't know what she means.

She thought about explaining what she meant, but decided she wasn't ready to hear the answer. The way Leon looked at her dad, she knew her parents already offered to let the sister move in. Out of the corner of her eye, she could see Jeremiah looking at her. She hoped the tears wouldn't fall. She didn't want him to know the thought of sharing her parents with another girl still upset her.

"Hey Dad," Jeremiah said. "I wonder if Griffin will confront Caleb's mom about lying."

Millie looked at him. Her brother was awesome. He winked at her and she knew he was changing the subject to get her out of an uncomfortable conversation.

"I imagine he will."

"Depending on what we find," Leon said, "there may be more criminal charges filed against the mom, too."

"Really?" Jeremiah said.

"I wouldn't doubt it," Leon pulled off the pavement and slowed to put the SUV into four-wheel-drive mode. "Sure, if she's lying to Griffin about the daughter, that means wherever the girl is probably isn't safe or it may involve her in illegal activities."

Millie felt her heart beat harder. She never thought about this girl being in danger. "Will she be in trouble if she is doing something illegal? Could she go to jail?"

“I don’t know the circumstances, but my guess is if she is doing something illegal, it’s probably against her will. She would be a victim, not a criminal.”

Millie’s hand went to her mouth and her breath came faster. All this time she only thought about herself. How selfish could she be? She looked over at Jeremiah. “This changes everything,” she whispered.

“What did you say, Millie?” Her dad turned to look at her.

“Oh, nothing, Dad.”

Chapter 62

Jeremiah

I knew once Millie realized Caleb's sister might be in trouble, most likely scared and mistreated, that she would want her to live with us. She didn't even have to say anything to me, I could read it in her eyes. I hoped that we would see the sister when we got up there. Even though Leon said we couldn't be there when he searched for her, what would he do if she was near the bumper when we got there?

"This is the way, right?" Leon said as he maneuvered around the rocks and bushes on the rutted road.

"Yes," Millie answered before I could. "About halfway up the hill. Look! You can see the sun shining on it right now."

"Isn't that something?" Dad said. "All this time Caleb knew what he was talking about, and we just thought it was a little kid rambling and confused."

"It's amazing what you learn from listening to children," Leon said.

"Have you had to listen to kids tell you stuff?" I asked.

"Twenty years in law enforcement, you better believe I've heard my share of stories from kids." Leon shook his head. "And most of them are not stories you'd want to hear."

"I'll bet your job is tough," Dad said.

Leon looked over at Dad, then glanced in his rearview mirror at both me and my sister. He was smiling. "It is, but there are good days, too. Like today. You've got some special kids there and because of them we might rescue another special kid."

Chapter 63

Millie

Millie tried not to sulk when Leon turned the car around and headed back down the hill. She had hoped they'd see the sister hanging around and could be there for the rescue.

"Millie," Jeremiah whispered.

Her dad and Leon talked about four-wheel-drive vehicles on the drive down the hill, a conversation that held no interest for her. They pulled back onto the pavement at the foot of the mountain when she looked over at Jeremiah. He pointed to the north.

A good distance ahead of them on the paved road was a big 18-wheeled mine truck. But this wasn't the road that led to the gypsum mine. What was it doing way out here? She and Jeremiah kept their eyes on the truck. As they got closer, Jeremiah whispered to her again. "It's the truck."

"What truck?" she mouthed. Her dad and Leon's conversation had tapered off, and she didn't want them to hear what they were saying. She pulled a notepad and pen from her backpack and handed it to her brother.

It's the one Mike and I saw the other night, he wrote.

Millie nodded and kept her eyes glued to the truck. It slowed and turned onto a dirt road.

She pointed to Jeremiah, but he was already watching it. He nodded. She wished her dad and Leon would start talking again so she and Jeremiah could talk. She picked up the pen and scribbled: *That road leads to the old store.*

Jeremiah nodded his head, then took the pad and pen from her. *And we're not going there!!!!*

Millie wished so hard that Paisley hadn't gotten sick. Paisley would have been willing to go with her. She had to know what was happening at the store and why that truck was heading there.

Then I'll go by myself!!!! she wrote and glared at Jeremiah when she showed it to him.

Millie watched him shake his head and stare out the side window. She could tell he was finished with this discussion. But she sure wasn't.

"Millie!" Mom was on the porch waiting for them when the car pulled up to the house.

Millie jumped out to greet her mother, wondering why she was so excited.

"Paisley is coming home!"

"Oh, Mom, I'm so glad!" Millie hugged her mom. "I thought they would be gone longer."

"They're eager to get back. Mrs. Morgan said they headed home as soon as they got out of the doctor's office. They should be here in about an hour and a half."

"I can't wait to see her. What did the doctor say? Is she okay?"

"Mrs. Morgan didn't say, and I didn't ask," Mom said.

"Why ever not?" Millie was too bold, as usual.

"Said the girl who won't ever stop asking questions." Jeremiah glared at her.

Millie snarled in return.

"They've been through a lot, Millie," Mom said. "They'll tell us when they're ready."

"Well, the fact that she didn't say everything is okay, tells me a lot." Millie's head dropped as she stepped through the front door.

A few minutes later she heard a knock on her bedroom door. "What?"

No answer. Just more knocking. Knocking that wouldn't quit. She stomped over to the door and jerked it open. "What?!" she said before it was all the way open. Then her mouth dropped. Jeremiah stood there in his riding gear, holding his helmet.

"What are you doing?"

"Come on, Mom said we can go back out and look for the meteorite for another hour."

"Really?"

"Yeah, really," Jeremiah stared at her. "And if we happen to look for something else while we're out there, maybe you'll cheer up."

Chapter 64

Jeremiah

"Why is Minnesota Mike parked over there in those trees?" Millie whispered as we sat on a hill overlooking the old store. For an abandoned store, there sure was a lot of activity at this one.

"Maybe for the same reason we're here watching. He seems to know there is stuff going on there. But he hasn't told me anything."

"He tried to chase down the truck that night," Millie said.

"That's true. So that's probably why he's watching it now, just like we are."

The mine truck we saw earlier was sitting with the engine idling in front of the store.

"I wonder if Mike sees us up here?"

"Maybe we should park somewhere else." Millie pulled out her kick starter. "I don't want him seeing us. He'll tell Mom and Dad."

I kicked over my bike and waited til Millie got hers started. She surprised me by taking the lead, so I followed, figuring this spy business was her idea. I was just along for the support or protection. Or maybe just so she wasn't the only one to get in trouble. Sheesh, sometimes it was hard to be a nice brother.

We pulled over near some trees close to the store.

"Let's leave the bikes here and get closer so we can see if that truck driver went into the store." Millie leaned her bike against the tree.

I wasn't thrilled with the idea of getting closer to that building, especially going in the back way, but I knew there was no stopping Millie now.

"Hopefully we don't run into Julia."

"I've been thinking about that, Millie. I don't see how she could do something illegal."

"I know. She seemed nice. And I can't figure a nurse who cares enough to go to someone's home to talk about their health, sneaking into an abandoned building."

"I wouldn't believe it if someone had told me."

Millie nodded her head. "Yeah, even seeing it, it's still hard to believe."

"Well, if she's here again today, then we definitely know she's not the person we thought."

"I would hate for Paisley's family to find out." Millie motioned me to follow. "Come on, let's get to the store before the truck drives off."

We followed along the same overgrown fence line, protected by the trees and shrubs, until we were close enough to see the truck. Millie stopped so suddenly I almost ran into her.

"Jeremiah," she whispered. "Look, there's a ladder leaned up against the truck."

"Maybe that's how the driver checks on stuff in those metal tanks." Even as I offered that lame suggestion, I knew it didn't sound right. I wondered if Minnesota Mike could see the truck and ladder from where he sat in his buggy. He'd probably have an idea what it was all about.

"Jeremiah, look!" Millie's whispers were getting louder, and that seemed dangerous.

I watched as a group of people streamed out the front door of the store and headed to the ladder. Millie gasped as we watched them one by one climb the ladder and disappear down into the metal tank of the truck.

"Smugglers, Millie." I couldn't believe what we were seeing. She never looked back at me or responded. She focused on a little girl crying at the foot of the ladder.

Chapter 65

Millie

"Ven rápida!" A woman's voice from the top of the ladder yelled at the young girl. Millie knew she was telling her to come quick. "Ven rápida!" This time the woman sounded angry. Millie watched as the little girl cried harder. "She's afraid to climb the ladder," she whispered. Without thinking, Millie darted from her hiding spot out to the girl and knelt on the ground, comforting her.

"Está bien," Millie whispered, "it's okay." She smoothed the girl's hair and held her close. "I'm here. Estoy aquí." She didn't look back at Jeremiah. She knew he'd be angry with her for doing this. But she couldn't let that child cry. She remembered too many days and nights when she was a young girl, crying and scared. She would have loved for someone to show up out of nowhere and comfort her. Like an angel. A guardian angel.

The girl clung to her and cried harder. Millie looked up and saw the angry woman at the top of the ladder disappear into the tank with the others.

"Oh, God," she prayed. "What have I done? What do I do now?" She had always been impulsive, but this was probably the most dangerous situation she had ever gotten herself into. Before she could make a choice, it was made for her.

A deep, angry voice from behind startled her. "Entre ahora!" She turned to face a large man pointing at the ladder. "Get in, now!"

Millie's heart beat hard as she stood and held onto the girl's hand. He must have thought she was with the rest of the group. She hesitated long enough for him to take a good look at her. He motioned to her boots, then stared at her riding apparel. She trembled as she recognized the man who threatened to handcuff her.

"Who are you?" his voice boomed, speaking only English now. She had no idea what to say, but a Bible verse popped into her mind. Do not worry about what you are to say, for it will be given you in that hour what you are to say. Oh, how she hoped that was true, even when she got herself in this dangerous situation.

The sudden roar of an engine took them by surprise and a red buggy charged in their direction. Millie grabbed the little girl and jumped out of the way as the buggy slammed into the ladder, knocking it to the ground. The loud crash intensified as the car drove over the fallen ladder, then circled the truck, coming back around again.

"Millie, run!" She heard Jeremiah's voice and without looking to see where the man was, still holding onto the young girl's hand, she ran faster than she ever had before, dragging the child along with her.

Chapter 66

Jeremiah

"¿Cuál es su nombre?" Millie knelt by the little girl and looked right in her eyes as she spoke to her.

Was this really happening? Did my sister really just rescue a little girl from smugglers? And surely this was the hand of God who rescued Millie.

Thankfully, Minnesota Mike was nearby for God to use. And how did Millie learn to speak Spanish? There was still a lot I had to learn about this sister of mine. Like where did she get this incredible courage to set her own safety aside to help a young child?

"My name is Mía," the girl said. "I know English."

"You do?" Millie sounded stunned.

Mía smiled, as if happy she surprised Millie. "I saw you before." She pointed at Millie.

"Me?" Millie stared at me, then looked back to Mía. "Where did you see me"

She pointed to the front of the store. "There. I saw you out the window."

Millie gasped. "I knew I saw movement in that window."

Wow, my sister was on to something even then and I thought she was just running off in a tangent.

"Where did you learn English?" I asked Mía.

She smiled at me and seemed to sense she was safe now. "The orfanato. A lady there teached it to me."

I looked at Millie. "What's an orfanato?"

"I think it means orphanage," Millie said. "She probably doesn't know that word in English."

"I didn't know you spoke Spanish, Millie."

She laughed. It didn't sound like one of her relaxed, carefree laughs though. I think the adrenaline was dwindling, and fear was setting in. "A little. They spoke Spanish at one of the foster homes where I lived."

"Did they teach it to you?"

"Ha!" Millie scoffed. "More like the other kids talked about me in Spanish, so I couldn't understand. That's why I learned some words, to figure out what they were saying."

She pulled a granola bar from her backpack and offered it to Mía. I watched as the bar disappeared. Mía chomped noisily, crumbs covering her mouth and cheeks. I wondered how long it had been since she ate.

We could hear the big truck driving away. I breathed a sigh of relief the man didn't follow Millie. I half expected to hear Minnesota Mike driving around looking for us, but it sounded like his buggy took off in the truck's direction.

"What do we do now, Jeremiah?" Millie looked like she could cry. It's funny how she could go from being so brave one minute, to being a scared little girl herself the next. That left me no choice.

"Let's take Mía home so Mom can feed her. She looks starved."

"What is Mom going to say? And Dad?" Now tears fell. "Oh, Jeremiah, what have I done?"

I couldn't help but laugh. "Well, you've topped yourself this time, Millie. I will say that." Mía listened to our conversation.

"Wrong or right, I think you've made a big difference in this little girl's life right now."

Millie took a deep breath. "You think so?"

I was almost tempted to hug my sister. Almost, but not quite. "I think so." I smiled and patted her on the shoulder.

Chapter 67

Millie

The ride home was slow with Mía on the back of Jeremiah's motorcycle. It was risky because they had no helmet for her. Millie chuckled at the thought of this being risky after what she had just gone through that brought Mía into their lives. She knew she would pay a big price for that risk later.

Their parents were out front watching for them when they pulled up. They both stepped off the porch, right over to Jeremiah's motorcycle, and greeted Mía as if they were expecting her.

"How did you know?" Millie said when she took her helmet off.

Dad lifted Mía off the bike.

"Minnesota Mike called and told us," Mom said.

"And then we called Leon." Dad set Mía on the ground and Mom knelt to greet her.

"Oh, no, Dad," Millie said. "Did you have to call him so soon?" She knew that meant they would come and take the little girl away. Somewhere that would be scary to her. Millie hoped she could spend a few days with them first.

"I told him about the mine truck and gave him Mike's number. Mike is following the truck. He's driving in the dirt alongside the highway, hanging back but keeping it in sight, until the Border Patrol gets there."

Millie's hopes rose. "So you didn't tell him about her?" Mía was already heading into the house with their Mom.

Dad smiled. "Not yet, Millie. I told him to stop by later so we could talk about something."

Millie threw her arms around him. "Thank you, Dad."

Jeremiah stepped up onto the porch and opened the door. Before he could get inside, Caleb rushed through the open door, running into Jeremiah. "Hey, who is that girl in there eating all our cookies? And where is my sissy? I thought you went to look for my sissy." His lip quivered, but he held back the tears.

"It's okay, big fella." Jeremiah sat on the porch step, pulling Caleb to his side. "Her name is Mía, and she's visiting us."

"But where is Jenny?"

"Jenny?" Millie took a seat on the porch step next to Caleb. "Is that your sister's name? You never told us before."

"I know." Caleb rubbed his eyes and hung his head down. "My mom told me I'm not supposed to talk about Jenny to anyone."

Millie locked eyes with her dad. She didn't know what to say.

Her dad knelt down. "It's okay, Caleb. Leon and Griffin are looking for Jenny, and you can talk about her now."

Caleb looked into their dad's eyes. "You won't tell my mom, will you? You know, my other mom, the one that went away."

Dad hugged him. "You don't have to worry about that anymore."

Mom and Mía joined them on the front porch. "Caleb, come and meet Mía. She's close to your age."

"I don't have to share my room with her, do I, Miss Norah?" He smiled up at her. "I mean Mom."

"Is she your mom?" Mía surprised Millie when she spoke to Caleb.

"Sure, she's my mom," Caleb stood and took Mom's hand. "If you want, she can be your mom, too. She's a good mom."

"Well, it isn't that easy, Caleb." Mom smiled at the boy. "Leon will help Mía find her mommy."

Mía smiled up at her. "I never had a mommy, Miss Norah."

Chapter 68

Jeremiah

Both Mom and Dad looked startled at Mía's comment, but before they could answer, Minnesota Mike's buggy roared in through our gate. We could hear him approaching the house, and I jumped up to greet him.

Paisley's family followed in their car. Millie flew off the porch steps. I watched as Paisley jumped out of the car just as fast. The girls hugged and cried. Sheesh. Girls.

I felt a small hand patting my leg and saw Mía looking at me. "Who are those people? Are they going to take me away?"

As much I would have liked for my parents to comfort her, they were both following Millie out to the car so I sat back down on the porch to look into Mía's eyes. "No, they won't take you. They'll be happy to meet you."

Mía smiled and followed me. Caleb and Donovan ran around chasing each other and laughing like they hadn't been together in weeks instead of just a couple days.

"Well, now if this ain't the purty little girl what Millie rescued." Minnesota Mike pulled his helmet off and joined them.

"Is he Santa Claus?" Mía whispered.

Mom rushed over and embraced Mike. "Thank you, thank you, thank you!" She wiped tears from her eyes. "I don't know what would have happened to Millie if you hadn't been there to intervene."

"Well, I'll tell ya." It looked like Mike was also wiping tears away. "I don't think I ever been so scared myself and," he pointed to Dad who had joined Mom. "It's your God, that One you been telling me about. That's the only reason I was in that spot this morning."

Paisley's parents joined us by Mike's buggy. "It sounds like we all have stories to share," her mom said. She was smiling, so it must be good news. At least I hoped so.

But then I saw Millie and Paisley talking, heads close together. When Millie threw her arms around Paisley and started crying again, I knew Paisley had already given her the news. And it sure didn't seem good.

Chapter 69

Millie

"Millie." Jeremiah startled her when he was so close. She wiped her eyes before looking his way. "Are you going to show Paisley our new pets?"

"Pets?" Paisley squealed. "You got pets? Plural, as in more than one?"

"Sixteen!" Caleb said. He looked at Donovan, eyes wide with excitement. "Lizards!"

"Lizards?" Mía screamed. "I hate lizards!"

"Where did she come from?" Paisley whispered. Millie, glad for the change in topic, put her arm around Mía and introduced her.

Minnesota Mike joined the girls. "You wouldn't believe what yer good friend did for this little gal."

Mom called out from the porch. "Let's all get some refreshments and share our stories."

"Well, how about this?" Mr. Morgan said. "We go away for a couple days and everything changes."

Mrs. Morgan sat with her arm around Millie while they all related the events of the morning. "God was surely watching over you today." She looked across the room, "And thank you Mike for being His instrument to care for her."

"I like the lizards best!" Donovan said. "I can't wait to hold one."

"It will be quite some time before those critters are ready to be held," Millie's Dad said. "They're angry now because of being mistreated."

"What about me?" Mía stood with her hands on her hips staring at the boys. "Aren't you excited about me?"

Millie hugged the girl and held back laughter at the look of horror on Caleb and Donovan's faces.

"The only girl I will get excited about," Caleb said, "is my sister Jenny. She'll be here soon."

"Leon is out looking for her, honey." Millie's mom smiled at Caleb. "We're not sure if he'll be able to find her."

"He'll find her, she lives by the light. She told me so."

This was news to all of them. "When did she tell you that, Caleb?" Jeremiah asked.

"I'll be right back, I gotta get something."

Millie followed Jeremiah to the hallway, curious to see what he was up to. He went into his room and came back out carrying his box of toy cars. Disappointed, Millie followed him back to the living room. She thought he had something to show them about his sister.

Caleb sat on the floor and spread the cars out near Donovan, then looked over at Jeremiah. "She came back to visit once and when my mom went outside, Jenny whispered and told me when I see the light shining on the hill, that she was there." He looked around the room at everyone staring at him. "And that's how I know."

Mía scooted over by the boys. "Can I play with the cars, too?"

"Oooh!" Caleb said. "Girls don't play with cars."

Mía reached for a bright blue car with orange decals. “I never had cars to play with.” She ignored the boys complaints and joined in.

“I had to get stucked with a needle today,” Donovan said to Caleb as they drove their cars around the chair on the far side of the living room.

“I hate needles.” Caleb chased Donovan’s car, overtaking him as they rounded the chair.

Millie looked over at Paisley. “I thought it was you they were checking out?” She turned to her mom and dad and saw a look of concern on their faces.

Paisley’s dad stood and motioned for them to follow. “How about if we go in the kitchen for some coffee?”

Millie knew there was a lot more than coffee drinking they were going in the kitchen for.

Chapter 70

Jeremiah

"Why did Donovan get stuck with a needle today?" Millie demanded in her typical rush-right-in-style as soon as we were all in the kitchen. Minnesota Mike offered to stay with the little ones in the living room. Who knows, maybe he'd rather play cars with them than face the news about Paisley. And now maybe even Donovan?

Mom set out cups, while Dad brought over the coffeepot as we gathered around the table. It's probably hard for a mom to hear another child might be in danger, and maybe that's why she busied herself getting cream and sugar and cookies and napkins. It was as if as long as she didn't sit down and look into the faces of Paisley and her parents, she didn't have to admit that her daughter's best friend might be in some danger.

I'm sure it wasn't far from her mind, the sad story Julia told about her children. Julia. I shuddered as I thought of her again. How was she involved in Mía being at the store?

Finally, Mom joined us at the table, and Mrs. Morgan broke the silence. It was amazing how long Millie waited for the answer to her question without demanding again to be told. But maybe, she, too, was afraid to hear.

"The doctor believes Paisley has the condition Julia told us about."

Mr. Morgan reached over and squeezed his wife's hand where it was resting on the table. I watched Millie's face go white. She avoided making eye contact with any of us, especially Paisley, sitting beside her. Millie, my tough-as-nails sister who just rescued a little girl from a smuggler, looked like she was ready to fall apart at this news about her best friend.

Paisley reached over and clasped Millie's hand, much the same way her dad did with her mother. Millie still refused to look at her. "There are treatments to keep me safe," Paisley said. "Julia most likely saved my life."

"Praise God for bringing Julia into our lives," Mom said.

"Amen," both Paisley's parents spoke at once.

"But why were they testing Donovan?" I repeated the question I knew Millie wondered about, but could no longer ask.

"Because it's very likely genetic, they tested all of us. We'll have the results in a few weeks," Mr. Morgan said.

"What led them to think that Julia may have been right?" Dad said.

"Paisley's electrocardiogram showed some irregularities, the kind typical with this condition. It's called Long QT Syndrome, and it's a problem with the electrical impulses the heart sends between heartbeats," Mrs. Morgan said.

The kitchen was quiet as we all took in the scary fact that Paisley could have died the day she passed out.

"Tell them about the treatment, Mom." Paisley, always the upbeat one, let go of Millie's hand and put her arm around her shoulders, squeezing her close. "It's okay, Millie, now that we know, the doctors can treat it. I will be fine. I can lead a normal life and still be as active as I want to be."

"Is that right?" Mom asked.

"Yes and no, Norah," Paisley's mom said. "A doctor will monitor her and they will treat it with medication. It's an excellent chance that she will be fine, but we have to be careful. I'm so very thankful for Julia."

"But you don't know the truth about Julia!" Millie blurted, startling everyone, especially me. We weren't supposed to talk about that until we found out why she had been at the store that day. Millie continued. "She's involved in the smuggling."

"Millicent!" Mom said.

"Now, hold on there, missy," Minnesota Mike's voice took us all by surprise. I sure hadn't seen him come into the kitchen. "You don't know what you're talking about."

Chapter 71

Millie

"Excuse me. I'll be right back." Millie stood and ignored the stares of everyone in the room, including Mike, as she passed him on her way out of the kitchen. Glad that the young ones were now in the playroom, she slipped out the front door with no one seeing her.

She felt so mature as she climbed the ladder to the tower. Just a few months ago she would have run off screaming or crying. This time she said "excuse me" before she left. It was almost funny. But she had no energy to laugh.

She winced at the memory of the time she ran crying far into their back acreage at night, climbed a hill, then fell and sprained her ankle and couldn't get back home. That was scary, listening to the coyotes howl. At least now she was more polite and stayed closer to home where it was safe.

Millie slumped down on the floor of the tower, hidden by the wooden walls her dad had built, and let the tears fall. This day was too much. First the poor lizards taped and stuffed in small containers, then finding Mía and that angry man scared her to death. Worst of all, finding out her best friend has something wrong with her heart. Something people, kids even, have died from. It was just all too much.

She laid down on the floor, her face buried in her hands, and let the tears flow.

"Millie?" The voice sounded far away. She didn't recognize it. "Millie?" It was a soft, comforting voice. Had she heard that voice before? She felt a hand touch her shoulder, then rub her back. "Millie? Can we talk?"

She struggled to open her eyes. Darkness surrounded her. How long had she been asleep?

Chapter 72

Jeremiah

"Jeremiah, why would your sister say such an outrageous thing about Julia?" Mom looked stunned.

That Millie. Well, she started it, so I'm just going to spill the beans on everything. That's what she gets for bringing up seeing Julia at the store and then taking off, leaving me here to answer the questions with a roomful of people staring at me.

"Jeremiah, do you know?" Dad said.

I guess all my thinking was taking too long. Well, here goes.

"Yes, I know." I took a deep breath and looked around the table. Minnesota Mike came the rest of the way into the kitchen and took a seat.

It's a weird feeling when you're getting ready to spill your guts and you know it will get you in lots of trouble. But I had no choice. Thank you, Sister Millie.

"We knew something strange has been going on at the old store for a couple weeks. So whenever we would go out riding, we would go by the store to see if we could see people there or what was happening."

"What do you mean something strange and what does this have to do with Julia?" Mom was just as bad as Millie with asking too many questions.

"Norah, give him a chance to explain."

Thank you, Dad.

With no more hesitating, I told them everything from the day Millie got handcuffed right up to seeing Julia and going back there today. Mom looked horrified, and Dad sat there shaking his head. I could just imagine the punishments they were lining up in their minds. We'd probably get grounded the rest of our lives.

"Well, I got to say that I'm a bit to blame here, too." Minnesota Mike's unexpected words interrupted the awkward silence.

It helped me out because everyone quit looking at me. It was like a ping-pong tournament, all the faces at the table turned away from me and toward Mike.

"I'm ashamed to say, I knowed about the trouble at the store when Millie got herself handcuffed and I shoulda told you."

Mom did not look happy hearing that confession. Maybe Mike would get grounded, too. I almost laughed out loud at that thought, but caught myself. Probably not a smart thing to do at a time like this. That's more like something Millie would do, except she was hiding somewhere and missing out on all this fun.

"Well, at first I didn't know fer sure, but I was up at the ice cream store about a week ago and I heard some fellers talking about some kids poking around the store. Heard 'em say something about handcuffing the girl to scare them away."

So that's how Mike knew. I wondered how he found out.

"Well, a few days later I sorta tricked Jeremiah into telling me it was them two at the store." He looked over at Dad and Mom with the sorriest look on his face I'd ever seen. "I never once thought them fool kids would go back there after a scare like that. I shoulda told you."

"Is that why you were there today?" Mom said.

"Well, now, ma'am," Minnesota said, "you know, I was sitting in my recliner watching an old black and white movie and then I just got the strangest urge to go fer a drive in my buggy. And once I got out there I saw that truck I suspected, so I started following it. And," he turned toward Mom, a pleading look in his eyes, "ya gotta believe me, I never in my wildest dreams expected to see your young'uns there at that store, too."

"Well, it was the hand of God that led you there, that's for sure," Dad said.

The sound of tires crunching on the gravel outside interrupted the conversation.

"Sounds like you've got more company," Mr. Morgan stood and motioned for his family to join him. "We'll go ahead and leave now. We've had a long day."

"Tell Millie I said goodbye," Paisley hugged Mom as she stepped away from the table.

Before any of us could get out the kitchen doorway, Caleb came barreling into the kitchen yelling for all the world to hear. "It's my sissy! Deputy Black has my sissy with him! Come on, everybody!"

Chapter 73

Millie

Millie opened her eyes, stunned to see the nurse sitting next to her on the tower floor. Julia smiled. "How could I ever have thought she was a bad person?" Millie wondered and felt shame looking into the gentle eyes.

"Julia?" She sat up and rubbed her eyes. Julia reached out and smoothed her hair, then leaned over and hugged her.

"Can we talk, Millie?"

"I'm so sorry." Millie felt tears welling up in her eyes again. She wondered if she would ever stop crying so much. "They must have told you what I said."

"Shh," Julia whispered. "It's okay."

"How can it be okay? I accused you of something so bad."

"It's okay because you did it out of love for the little ones like Mía. You weren't being mean just for the sake of being mean. You care so much for others and you want to heal their hurts." Julia smiled. "You're very special, Millie. You risked your own life to save hers."

"I'm not sure it was the smartest thing I've ever done, but it worked out."

"Yes, it was dangerous and I'm sure Leon will talk about that with you, but for now, look how wonderful it turned out for little Mía." Julia clapped her hands together. "Now, let me tell you why I was at the store that morning."

"So it was you?" Millie asked.

"Yes, and my husband Tucker." Julia beamed. "When I went home the other evening and told him that the store I have such fond memories of was for sale, he wanted to go see it."

Millie couldn't believe what she was hearing.

"Tucker has been wanting me to change careers."

"He doesn't like you being a nurse?"

"Well, not that so much, as the environment I've worked in for some time has been hostile. To me, at least."

"Is that why you couldn't talk about the heart condition with Paisley's mom at the hospital."

"Yes, it is."

"Does that mean you are buying the store?"

Julia's broad smile answered that question. "We just came from visiting Paisley's family and telling them the news."

Millie got on her knees to peer over the wall of the tower, looking for Paisley's car. "Did they go home?"

Julia laughed. "Quite some time ago. I'm told you've been out here sleeping for several hours. Did you know it's almost ten o'clock?"

"Oh no, I've missed everything. Did Leon ever come back? What about Caleb's sister?"

Chapter 74

Jeremiah

I knew as soon as I saw this girl she was nothing, and I mean nothing like Millie. Caleb clung to her like he hadn't seen her in years. And who knows, maybe he hadn't? She hugged him back just as hard and I wondered where has she been living and what's been going on in her life? Her hair looked like she didn't own a brush and not sure the last time they washed her clothes. But the biggest contrast between her and Millie was how timid she was.

Mom embraced the two kids. Caleb wiggled out of Mom's arms, then grabbed hold of her hand and his sister's hand. "Jenny, this is our new mom. Her name is Norah." I saw Mom turn and look at Dad and then Deputy Black.

Jenny didn't even look at Mom. "Where is our mom?" she whispered to Caleb. Millie would be glad to know I stood close enough to hear what they were saying so I could pass the info along to her.

"She's gone away somewheres," Caleb said.

"I hope she went to jail." Jenny still whispered, looking only at her brother.

He seemed surprised. "Jenny? Why would you say that?"

Jenny didn't answer. Just stood there and cried. Uh-oh. She had at least one of Millie's characteristics. But crying wasn't as bad as being pushy.

Mom put her arm around Jenny. "Honey, let's go in the house and get you something to eat."

I never saw Paisley's family leave. They must have slipped out the back door which probably was best. I think it would have been even harder on Jenny for so many people to be here. Caleb looked torn between following Mom and Jenny inside or staying outside. He looked up at me. "Why did she say our mom should go to jail?"

"Hey buddy," Deputy Black rescued me. "Jenny's upset. She's tired and hungry and scared." He knelt down and looked into Caleb's eyes. "We all say things when we're feeling overwhelmed." He hugged Caleb. "Do you know what I mean?"

"I guess so. But I told her we got a new mom now." He looked into Deputy Black's eyes, then over at Dad. "She can live here too, can't she?"

CHAPTER 75

Millie

"We should go in the house quietly," Julia followed Millie down the ladder.

Millie looked up at her, puzzled.

"Jenny and Caleb are asleep on the couch."

"She's here? They found her? Why didn't anyone tell me?"

"So many questions, girl." Julia tucked her arm around Millie shoulders when she reached the ground. "Your parents just wanted to let you sleep, you were exhausted and upset. And honestly, so was Jenny they tell me."

"You didn't talk to her?"

Julia took Millie by the hand and headed to the garden. "Let's chat for a bit and I'll tell you what I learned."

Millie grabbed her stomach at the loud growl. "I think I slept through dinner."

"It sure sounds like it." Julia laughed as they both took a seat on the garden bench.

"My husband and I went to visit Paisley's family after we left the realtor's office late this afternoon. I wanted to hear about Paisley's test results and tell them our news about the store."

"So Paisley already knows? Was she happy about it?"

"Oh yes, very and especially her parents. I'll be close by and able to help them learn about living with Paisley's condition."

"And if there's an emergency?"

"Well, I'm not a doctor, but I can be there until they get medical attention." Julia nodded. "But with proper treatment and monitoring any symptoms, I'm not expecting any emergencies."

"I'm so glad," Millie said. "I was worried about her. Did you know I never had a best friend in my life until I met Paisley?"

"You two are perfect for each other." Julia patted Millie's knee. "And I think you'll be a perfect friend for Jenny, too."

"What were you going to tell me about her?"

"Leon and Griffin found her living in a shack close to where you two found the box this morning."

"Oh, no, that's awful." Millie felt ashamed of her earlier selfish thoughts about not wanting the sister to live with them.

"Her mother was getting paid for Jenny to live there and help with the smuggling of the reptiles. Before they started using drones, it was Jenny's job to signal the pilots of the planes. That's what the bumper was for, to reflect the sun so the pilots knew where to make the drop. Then she would get the boxes."

"Did she know what was in them?" Millie felt sick at the news.

"Griffin doesn't think she knew what was in the boxes or that it was smuggling. She just knows her mom was making her live there and work for the couple. She got paid a little, but Griffin and Leon think her mom was getting most of the money."

Another long growl from Millie's stomach distracted them. "We better get you inside to eat." Julia stood and pulled Millie up with her.

Millie stretched and rubbed her rumbling stomach, then headed toward the house. She looked over at Julia as they walked. "So how did you come to be over here so late, anyway?"

She regretted asking that question when she heard the answer.

“Paisley’s family told me you thought I was involved with the smugglers.”

Millie felt her ears burning. “I’m so sorry.” She kept her head down, unable to face Julia.

“It’s okay.” Julia put her arm around Millie’s shoulders as they walked. “I just wanted to clear that up right away and your parents said it was okay for us to stop by after we left Paisley’s.”

“Millie! There you are!” Mom’s enthusiasm warmed Millie’s heart as she stood waiting on the porch with open arms.

Chapter 76

Jeremiah

"This house is filling up with kids faster than I thought it could happen." The smile on Griffin's face as he came through the door followed by Leon gave me some sense of relief. When Mom and Dad told us they were coming over this morning to talk to me and Millie, I had an uncomfortable feeling. I doubted this time it would be to tell us about a big reward like before.

Mía and Caleb bickered over the toy cars. Poor Caleb. Mía was like a miniature Millie. Give up now, kid, I felt like telling him. You don't even have a chance. Jenny sat on the floor next to her brother, whispering to him. Caleb didn't look happy about whatever she said, but I saw him let go of the car Mía wanted.

Minnesota Mike sat on the couch chuckling about it all.

"Jeremiah, Millie." Dad motioned for us to follow him. "Let's go in the kitchen and chat with the officers while Mike watches the kids."

Uh-oh, he called them officers. That sounds so much more formal than calling them by their names. I thought they were our friends. Officers? I wondered if we were in trouble. By the look on Millie's face, she must have been thinking the same thing.

"How are those lizards doing?" Leon looked over at Millie as he took a seat at the table. Mom sat cups of coffee on the table but gave Leon iced tea. I noticed she didn't put out any cookies or muffins. So definitely not a social call. Come on, Millie, I thought, tell him about the stupid lizards so we can get on with the bad news. If I had said that, Millie would have had a fit because I called them stupid.

"They're doing good."

A three word answer? Not like her at all. Definitely nervous.

"Well, kids," Leon looked from Millie to me. "Some good things have come out of the risks you've taken. Mía and Jenny were rescued." He smiled, but not too big, I noticed. Mom and Dad stayed quiet. I'm sure they'd have plenty to say later.

"The reptile smuggling ring has been discovered."

"Julia said Jenny didn't know about the lizards." Millie's curiosity must have overcome her fear.

"That's true," Leon said. "She thought the dropped boxes were supplies. It was her job to retrieve the boxes." He paused and took a long drink of his iced tea.

"But you took risks." Now he wasn't smiling. "Serious ones. You could have been hurt or worse."

It was hard to make eye contact with Leon while he spoke, and no way could I look at our parents. Silence filled the room. I couldn't even hear the other kids. Mike must have taken them outside.

"Do you remember when I told you to report any suspicious activity to me?" Leon was stern.

"I do."

"Did you do that?" Leon looked over at Millie. "Either of you?"

We were both speechless, at least I assumed Millie was, I sure heard nothing from her and I couldn't take my eyes off Leon. I shook my head.

"It's your decision," Leon looked at my parents, "but I'd recommend that they not leave the property for a few weeks, maybe longer."

"Absolutely," Dad and Mom both said at the same time.

"And when you go riding again off your parent's property," Leon looked back at both of us. "Only ride between here and Ridge Riders Lodge, or over in the off road park. There are park rangers over there. No going back to those hills south of here."

"Okay." We both spoke at the same time.

"You two are awesome kids." Griffin smiled. Wow, what a relief. Leon nodded his head at Griffin's words. "You're curious, you're adventurous, you're brave. Maybe a little too brave." It seemed funny, but I didn't know if it was okay to laugh. "Leon is right, when you see something suspicious, never investigate yourself. Tell your parents and contact us."

"Besides the risks you took," Dad said, "there was a fair amount of dishonesty going on too."

"Dishonesty?" Millie asked what I wondered about.

"Didn't you tell us each time you went riding this last week that you were searching for a meteorite?" Mom did not sound happy. "Whatever happened to that plan?"

Chapter 77

Millie

"Why do you think Jenny didn't want to roast marshmallows with us?" Millie dangled her stick in the fire, letting the marshmallow flare, before pulling it back out.

"She's probably scared. She doesn't know us."

"Do you think Mom will make her do schoolwork? And Mía?" She pulled the way too hot marshmallow off the stick, wincing when it burnt her fingertips.

"You're not going to put that in your mouth right away, are you?" Millie was bouncing it around with her tongue before Jeremiah even got the words out. She gasped for cool air and waved her hand in front of her mouth. Jeremiah shook his head like he thought she wasn't too smart.

"Well, are they?" Her words were garbled, coming from her marshmallow filled mouth.

"Are they what?" He lifted his roasting stick out of the fire, waving his marshmallow around in the cool air.

"Are they going to be doing schoolwork?"

"Millie, you heard Mom and Dad. They don't even know how long the girls will be here. You don't just find kids and bring them home and keep them."

"Yeah, but you know Mom and Dad," Millie shoved another marshmallow on the end of the stick. "They'll make this work somehow. You can tell, both those girls need a home."

"Not my problem whether or not they do schoolwork." Jeremiah popped his barely browned marshmallow into his mouth.

Why he couldn't roast them to a decent brown, she just couldn't understand. "Well, it isn't fair."

"What isn't?" He stared at her like he had no clue what she was talking about.

"It isn't fair if they're doing nothing, while we're doing school. I mean, if it wasn't for us, they wouldn't even be here."

"Sounding a little boastful there, aren't you?"

She had to admit it didn't sound like the right thing to say. "I guess what's bothering me the most." She stopped to focus on shoving three marshmallows on the end. "Why is Mom making us do that stupid 15 page report on meteors on top of all our regular schoolwork?"

"Millie, I think we got off pretty easy with what we did. I mean, for one thing, we're still alive in spite of all those dangerous risks. For another, they could have taken our motorcycles away for good."

"But why a report on meteors? I don't even care about them."

"Well, maybe because that's what we were supposed to be searching for, the meteorite that fell to the ground last week."

She saw Jeremiah watching as she waved the flaming stick around. She thought about shoving all three hot marshmallows in her mouth at once just to annoy him. But she figured that might hurt. Instead, she put the stick back in the fire and let them burn.

"Look at it this way," he said. "Maybe we'll learn something about hunting for meteorites and we can find it when we're allowed to go out riding again."

"Yeah, I guess that sounds like a good idea. I wonder if we can sell it when we find it, and get rich? Or famous? Yeah, we can get famous. Those professor dudes will be so excited when we contact them." She shoved four marshmallows on the stick.

"Don't fill that whole stick." Jeremiah grabbed the bag from her. "In the meantime, maybe we can get off the property by offering to help Julia and Tucker clean up the new Dry Brook Trading Post."

"Wait a minute, what happened to calling it Ye Olde Dry Brook Trading Post."

"That's the old name." Jeremiah popped the lightly roasted marshmallow into his mouth. "This is the new Dry Brook Trading Post. That's what Julia told us when you were hiding out in the tower."

"So how did Minnesota Mike know about Julia and her husband buying that store, anyway?"

"You missed out on that when you ran off."

"I didn't run." Millie shook her finger at her brother. "I politely excused myself."

"I guess you're right," Jeremiah said. "Well, turns out it was Minnesota Mike's idea all along. He met Julia when he was in the hospital and knew she wasn't happy in her job. Once he found out the store was for sale, he started checking to make sure no one had put an offer on it. The realtor told him the place had been deserted for years with no interest from anyone."

Jeremiah stood and stretched, then sat back down. "That explained why when he and I drove by the store, he knew no one should have been there."

"So, how did he know Julia and her husband bought the store? You haven't even answered that question in that long history lesson."

"Remember at Paisley's house when he hinted to Julia about the right person buying the store?"

"Yeah."

"When they went out in the buggy he drove her to the store and talked to her about his idea. He said he was even more sure it was the right thing to do when he learned she had gone there as a kid. So Minnesota Mike was the first one she told after they worked out the deal."

"Wow," Millie said, staring into the fire. "The things you miss when you get upset and walk out on everybody."

"Hey."

Millie and Jeremiah both jumped at the sound of a voice near the garden. They stood and looked around.

A boy about Jeremiah's age stood near Millie's rock formation, barely discernible in the dim firelight.

"Where did you come from?" she said.

He took a few steps toward the fire. "Is this the place that takes in kids?"

Millie looked at Jeremiah. His eyes were as wide as hers felt. "What should we do?" she said.

"What do you think?" Jeremiah looked at her like she was brainless. "We need to go tell Mom and Dad about this right away."

"Be right back, kid," Millie said, and they took off running for the house.

Acknowledgements

It takes the help of many people to bring a story to life. I am grateful to my family members who patiently listen to never-ending talk and questions about my book adventures. They offer suggestions and are the first readers, providing valuable feedback:

Summer, age 14, Granddaughter – First Reader
Jana Foley, Aunt – Second Reader
Steve Kukla, Husband – Third and Most Critical Reader

For helping with accuracy and authenticity in this book, thank you Jolene Crouse, RN with Palomar Health in San Diego County (who also races her quad in the desert) and Terri Peterla, middle school teacher at New Hanover Township School in Wrightstown NJ. These ladies gave their time to read the manuscript while it was still a work in progress, then provided feedback and answered questions, to help with the final editing.

Thank you to my sister and brother-in-law for prayer support and encouragement: Regina and Alan Jensen; to my grandson, Wyatt Kukla, age 7, who loves previewing and helping choose book covers.

I am especially grateful to the members of the LQTS Kids & Families Facebook page who gave valuable input: Shelby Nicole Balk, Thomson IL; Stephanie Lentell, Port Orchard WA; Melissa Marie, Ohio; Eileen Pike, Westchester NY; Jan Schiller, SADS Foundation, www.sads.org; Dianna Walters, St. Louis MO; Jasmine Wylie, San Francisco CA; and Amy Whittle, teacher, Idalou Middle School, Idalou TX.

Thank you Christine Puricelli, mother of Emilie, to whom the book is dedicated, for providing these resources to learn about children and adults who may be at risk for heart related sudden death: Parent Heart Watch, www.parentheartwatch.org; Mayo Clinic (search Long QT Syndrome), www.mayoclinic.org; SADS Foundation, www.sads.org and Sudden Cardiac Arrest Association, www.suddencardiacarrest.org

Read Emilie's story at
www.sads.org/healing-wall-entries/Emilie-Puricelli

Lastly, I give all praise to God, the Creator, for blessing us with creative abilities and for His wondrous gift of salvation and abundant life.

Will you help promote MotoMysteries with a review of *Ghost Lights of Dry Brook?*

Online reviews play a big role in the success of a book. Many readers choose what book to order based on what reviewers have to say. If you could take a few minutes and give an honest review at one or all of the following websites, I'd be very grateful.

Amazon.com
BookBub.com
Goodreads.com

Thank you and thanks for coming along on Jeremiah and Millie's adventures!

Sherri Kukla

Sherri Kukla
sherrikukla@gmail.com

P.S. If you'd like, send me an email after you leave a review! I'd love to hear from you and to go on-line and read the review!

ABOUT THE AUTHOR

Sherri Kukla and her husband Steve are the publishers of *S&S Off Road Magazine* and the founders and directors of Thundering Trails off road camp for kids. They reside in the off road community of Ocotillo Wells CA with their teenage granddaughter and a dozen or so motorcycles, surrounded by coyotes, snakes, rabbits and other desert critters.

Have you read these MotoMysteries books?

Book 1 – *The Skeleton and the Lantern*
Book 2 - *Ghost Lights of Dry Brook*
Book 3 - *Phantom Ship in the Desert* (Fall 2020)

The Christmas Miracle
A Christmas Mini-Mystery

Available in print and ebook on Amazon

www.sherrikukla.com
www.facebook.com/motomysteries

Made in the USA
Columbia, SC
14 June 2020